SHIFTY

SHIFTY

LYNN E. HAZEN

Tricycle Press
Berkeley

Text copyright © 2008 by Lynn E. Hazen
Cover photo copyright © 2010 by Veer.com/PhotoAlto Photography

Published in the United States by Tricycle Press, an imprint of the Crown Publishing Group, a division of Random House, Inc., New York.
www.crownpublishing.com
www.tricyclepress.com

Tricycle Press and the Tricycle Press colophon are registered trademarks of Random House, Inc.

Library of Congress Cataloging-in-Publication Data

Hazen, Lynn E.
    Shifty / by Lynn E. Hazen.
        p. cm.
    Summary: Fifteen-year-old Soli, nicknamed Shifty, keeps getting into trouble without trying, but as he strives to trust and be trusted, he grows in appreciation of his foster family and works toward putting his past behind him. [1. Foster home care—Fiction. 2. Trust (Psychology)—Fiction. 3. Family life—California—San Francisco—Fiction. 4. Conduct of life—Fiction. 5. San Francisco (Calif.)—Fiction.] I. Title.
    PZ7.H314977Shi 2008
    [Fic]—dc22

                        2007046363

ISBN 978-1-58246-257-8 (hardcover)
ISBN 978-1-58246-322-3 (paperback)

First Tricycle Press printing, 2008
Printed in USA

Design by Katy Brown
Typeset in Scala, Franklin Gothic, and Boycott

1 2 3 4 5 6 — 14 13 12 11 10

First Paperback Edition

The truth of this fictitious story is dedicated with love to my mom, and to all the rest of us brave moms who have to let go; and to our independent offspring who keep getting in those cars and driving away, with—rightly so—barely a glance in the rearview mirror.

Wear your seat belts everybody!
Adjust those mirrors from time to time.
Drive carefully.

Shifty is also dedicated to the many children and youth still yearning for a home, still searching for a home within.

CHAPTER 1

Summer is just starting and I'm getting into trouble without even trying. Just like the summer I got sent to juvie. Only none of that was my fault. Now it's happening all over again. I park the van for just a second in the bus zone on Mission Street. I need to buy me a burrito after the last day of school. I look first—and there's no bus coming. But cops are always looking too. Looking for guys like me.

When I come out with my burrito the cop is gone, but the ticket is right there on Martha's windshield. At least no one wants to see my driver's license—the license I don't have.

"Expensive burrito," Martha says when I get back. Two hundred and seventy-five bucks Martha has to pay for that ticket. She says I owe it to her now, and I got to repay her—one way or another.

"Why'd you get a burrito anyway?" Martha asks. "We're going to Hong Sing's tonight."

"I was hungry," I say.

Martha usually splurges on Friday nights with Chinese takeout. Sissy holds the door open at Hong Sing's for Martha and the baby. I'm already inside, checking out the specials and taking a number so we won't have to wait all night. I like the steamy windows in this crowded place, the sizzling garlic smell, and the yelling back and forth.

"The Hong Sing special ribs look good," I say.

"I know, Soli," Martha says. "But I've still got some food in the fridge at home."

Martha must be worried about that expensive bus zone ticket because she only orders half as much as usual—just pot stickers and the green bean garlic chicken. Back at Martha's the pot stickers are perfect. The garlic chicken and Martha's leftovers aren't bad either. One thing about Martha is, she doesn't skimp on meals. The food might not all match up, like tonight's Chinese takeout, leftover hot dogs, and canned beans—but for the ten months or so I've been here, there's always been plenty of it. Not like some places I've lived, where they put locks on the refrigerator and cupboards and you got to listen to your empty stomach grumbling all day and night.

Sissy eats head-down, silent as usual, with one hand in her sweater pocket. But she perks up a little at the fortune cookies.

I open mine first.

"What's it say?" Martha asks.

"*A sly rabbit has three openings to its den.* Whatever that's supposed to mean."

Sissy looks at hers but it's got too many words. She hands it to Martha.

"*Keep a green tree in your heart and a songbird will come.*" Martha pats Sissy's hand, then gives the fortune back. Sissy tucks it into her pocket.

"You both did better than me," Martha says. "Listen to this: *You will come to the attention of those in authority.* I hope not. That's the last thing I need."

Martha crumples her fortune and tosses it in the trash. I should have paid more attention. Because Martha and me, maybe we got our fortunes crossed.

A few days later, I'm minding my own business, staying out of trouble, looking for another parking place—this time at that new Mission shopping center. You'd think it wouldn't be so crowded on a weekday morning. You'd think a big city like San Francisco could create more parking spots.

I look for a parking space while watching out for "authorities." I see a cop in front of the Jamba Juice a couple of stores down from Toy Mart and Rite Aid. So Sissy and me, we're stuck driving around and around that lot with no place to park. It's not my idea to take Sissy shopping. But Sissy's never been to any birthday party and all of a sudden she's invited—Sissy's so nervous about it in her no-talking, no-smiling, watching-everything, seven-year-old-self kind of way. And Martha says I have to take my little sister to the store to help her choose a present for her new school friend. Well Sissy, she's not my real sister. And Martha, she's not my real mom either. But I have to do it because "we got to help each other out," Martha says, and now she's so busy with that new crack baby.

"He's not a crack baby," Martha tells me. "He's a baby first. A baby born addicted to drugs."

Pitiful, the way he shakes and all, and I doubt he's got a chance in this world, but no use telling that to Martha. Martha believes in lost causes like Sissy and that scrawny little baby-first crack baby.

Sissy is not her real name, but she wants to be called Little Sister or Sissy all the time. And according to Martha, Sissy and I are not "foster kids" either. We are "kids first." She makes us repeat her "people first" language, and now it's starting to stick in my brain. Sissy and me, we are "kids living in a foster home." Not foster kids. Nope, not according to Martha.

There's still no place to park. But that cop finally disappears, so I pull into the handicapped zone in front of Toy Mart. We're only going to be here a few minutes, and besides, I'm staying in the van. Martha told me and Sissy to walk to one of those cheap stores on Mission

Street and "hurry back." But walking would've taken too long. The fastest thing to do was borrow her van. Plus, I want to look at the radar detectors at the auto-supply store on the way back. Martha lets me drive her old van, especially when I'm late for school, or her knee is sore, or that jittery baby won't stop crying. Of course, she usually comes along for the ride.

I like how Martha is all trusting of me. Not too many people trust me like that. No one besides Martha, in fact. I got a whole file full of people saying how I'm shifty and not to be trusted. But Martha, she trusts the good in people, even when the bad part is showing up more than anything else.

When I first came to Martha's house, she asked me if I had a driving permit. I said yeah. She never asked if the permit had my name on it, or if I was old enough to drive. I'm old enough. Just not according to the State of California.

So I can't exactly tell Martha that the permit isn't mine. It's not my fault I'm tall and I look older than fifteen. I was just helping out Wired at my last group home. He needed all the help he could get. I took the written test for him at the DMV and I only got three wrong. Wired never would've passed. He was so grateful he gave me a copy of his permit. Of course the permit has Wired's name on it—his real name, Franklin. The flimsy black-and-white photo is faded and doesn't look much like me unless I tilt my chin up and smile with all my teeth showing, just like Wired does. Luckily Martha's eyesight isn't all that good.

And now, with her leg bothering her, it seems a shame to all of a sudden tell Martha that I can't get my own real permit until I'm fifteen and a half. That's five months from now. I like driving and I'm good at it. Besides, Martha keeps saying she needs my help since she's so busy with that jittery baby-first crack baby. And I'm not the only one bending the rules. I looked in Martha's wallet. Her license is expired too.

I don't want to get another ticket, so I plan to take Martha's blue handicapped tag out of her glove box and hook it on the rearview mirror. With her knee swollen most of the time and the bottom half of her left leg missing all the time, Martha has a right to those handicapped spaces. Martha usually keeps her blue tag in the glove box and pretends she's just fine. Like if she pretends she's fine, no one will notice she's got a fake leg below her knee. Her prosthesis, she calls it.

"I get around," she says. "I get around just fine."

Yeah, I could've parked farther away like Martha usually does. But the way I see it, she's wasting a perfectly good blue tag, and those parking spaces are empty most of the time anyway. That's what I'm thinking when I pull into the handicapped space up front. Sissy gives me one of those sideways looks of hers, but she doesn't say a thing.

I stay in the van and send skinny-legged Sissy in with her ten dollars scrunched in her fist. I'll watch for cops—and if anyone really handicapped comes along, of course I'll move the van. But Sissy, she takes too long. And when she comes back out, she's empty-handed.

"What?" I ask her.

Sissy shrugs and slides her hands into her sweater pockets.

"Where's the present?"

She looks down, then back at the store.

"You better hurry up," I say. "Or I'm leaving."

"What if . . . ," she stops mid-sentence.

"What if what?"

"What if . . . I get the wrong thing?" she says.

That's a lot of words from Sissy. She's been at Martha's three months now, and she barely says more than three words at a time.

So I tell her, "Choose something you'd like for yourself, and your friend will like it just fine. And hurry up while you're at it."

I listen to four or five more songs on the radio. But Sissy's not hurrying. She doesn't even come back out. So I have to go check on her. That's what big brothers are supposed to do, right?

I find her standing in the dollhouse aisle, but she's not looking at baby dolls or doggies or toy cars or furniture. Nope—she's got a row of little plastic mamas lined up. A brown mama, a black mama, and a white mama. She can't decide which.

I tell her, "The brown mama's good—it looks like a skinny version of Martha."

I switch some price tags around so we'll get more change and we buy it quick, but not quick enough. As soon as we're out of the store, I see I forgot to hang Martha's blue handicapped tag on the mirror. Sissy should have reminded me, because now that Jamba Juice cop is right in front of Martha's van. And she's pulling out her pad, all ready to write me a ticket.

So of course, I have to stop her.

CHAPTER 2

I run up to the van and start talking.

"Good morning, Officer," I say.

She hasn't started writing the ticket yet.

"My little sister and I are heading home. Get in, Sissy," I say.

Sissy, she comes up real slow. She's silent, squeezing her bag with that new plastic mama inside. Sissy's got the right idea. Why didn't I keep quiet? Too late now.

"This your car?" the cop asks me.

"Yes, ma'am," I say. I unlock the front passenger door, and Sissy gets in.

The cop looks me up and down. She doesn't trust me, I can tell.

"You know you're in a handicapped zone?"

"Yes, ma'am. My mama's handicapped. She's in the Rite Aid, buying a lot of stuff. I better go help her."

Sissy's eyes get big, but she's not saying a word. That's one of the good things about Sissy.

"Sissy, look—you forgot to put Mama's sign on the mirror!" I reach into the glove box and pull out Martha's handicapped tag. But I can tell that cop isn't satisfied and she's not putting her ticket pad away either. I'm thinking about Martha and how I already owe her two hundred and seventy-five bucks for the last ticket.

This cop might ask to see my license. That'd be bad. And I'm not supposed to drive Sissy around by myself. Besides that, only Martha is authorized to use the blue tag.

"I better go help my mama," I say.

I leave Sissy where she is and walk into the drugstore. I look out the window, waiting for the cop to move on, but the clerk keeps eyeballing me.

He comes up and says, "Can I help you?"

He doesn't want to help me. He wants me to steal something so he can call security.

"No thanks," I say.

I peer through the dusty window display, and that's when I see her—the old lady walking along with her arms full of bags. She looks like she's wearing all the clothes she owns and she's lugging bags full of bottles, newspapers, and stuff.

I leave the store, but the cop is still there—ready to write me a ticket. And Sissy's sitting in the van all quiet. Martha's back at the house, rocking and singing to that shaky new baby, I'm sure. She's trusting me. And me? I'm messing up, as usual.

The lady with too many bags is walking slowly—closer and closer to the van.

So, what do I do?

I shout, "Mama, there you are. Let me help you with those bags."

And that raggedy lady squints like she's trying to recognize me. But of course she doesn't.

"This is your mama?" the cop asks me. She looks back and forth between me and the old lady.

That old lady's got deep wrinkles like someone ironed them in. Her gray hair is sticking out of a purple flowered scarf. The scarf isn't too clean and she looks kind of dazed.

"Actually, she's my grandma, but everyone calls her 'Mama.' Isn't that right, Mama?"

"Is this your grandson, ma'am?" asks the cop.

The old lady doesn't answer. I bet that cop is wondering why I don't look anything like her. But hey, this is San Francisco and they got all kinds of different-looking people here. Sissy's sitting in the front seat getting silenter and silenter.

"Mama," I say. "You ready?"

I slide open the door to the backseat. That lady lets me take her bags and says, "Thank you, son."

She climbs in and I help her with the seat belt, even though she smells a little. I jam her bags in there too. And Sissy, her eyes couldn't get any bigger. She doesn't look at the backseat. She doesn't look at the cop who's shaking her head and gazing up at the sky like it might rain any minute. But I look at the whole situation as I slide the door closed. I ease into the driver's seat. I see that cop finally tuck her ticket pad away, and then I look at myself in the rearview mirror—me without a ticket.

I put my seat belt on, shift into reverse, and I back out real careful.

We are out of there.

When we pull out of the parking lot with no ticket, I am so happy I thump on the steering wheel. I haven't been this happy in a long time. But Sissy doesn't look too pleased. She steals a quick glance at me.

"Don't worry," I say. "Martha's not going to find out."

It starts drizzling, so I turn on the wipers. We drive a couple of blocks with the radio turned low and those wipers going *swush-swush* real slow, and that parking lot getting farther and farther behind us. The lady in the backseat starts to hum a little, but not exactly along with the music.

Sissy keeps facing front but she slides her eyes—those dark brown eyes—sideways at me and whispers, "Where we taking your new grandma?"

CHAPTER 3

Sissy doesn't talk much, but I guess her brain's always thinking.

I look in the rearview mirror and I say to the lady, "Thanks for helping me out back there. You saved me a lot of trouble."

"Heavy bags," the raggedy lady says. "Weighing me down, weighing me down."

"Just tell me which way to go," I say. "And I'll take you home."

"Home?" the lady says, like she's asking herself a question. Then she directs me every which way like she forgot where she lives.

Now we're driving in an area that doesn't look so safe. The radio commercials are getting louder and louder and the van is starting to smell. If we don't drop off this bag lady and get back quick, Sissy's going to miss her party and Martha's bound to ask questions. She'll figure out I took her van. More papers will be added to my file and I'll be switched to another foster home, just like before, and before that, and before that.

Martha never should have trusted me.

They'll take away Wired's expired permit. I'll never get a license or my own car, or take that road trip with Wired we mapped out. My plan of chowing down and laying low at Martha's till I find Wired again is never gonna happen. They'll put my name in some computer database for troublemaking kids, maybe send me off to some work camp. "Shifty kid," they'll say. "Shifty, good-for-nothing kid."

That's what happened that time with Janice and J.J. and his stupid knife. I had nothing to do with any of that. And the summer with Pat and Louise—how was I supposed to know what they kept in their glove box? But I still got hauled in to juvie. Just thinking about it makes my hands tighten on the steering wheel.

Finally the lost lady in the backseat stops humming. "Let me out," she says. "Right here on the corner."

It's hard to get her and her bags out of the van and Sissy refuses to help. After the old lady finally wanders off toward those warehouses, I open all the windows with the power switch for some fresh air. A little drizzle won't hurt Martha's peeling upholstery. Sissy's been looking straight ahead. But now she turns and glares at me. Then she turns her whole body around and looks behind us. She watches that raggedy lady disappear.

"No telling any of this to Martha," I say. "Okay?"

Sissy keeps looking behind us—like there's a movie playing in the back window.

"It's raining," Sissy says. "She's getting all wet."

"She'll be fine. She's right near her home."

"No home," Sissy says.

"Sure, she's got a home. She told us where to let her off."

"She's got nowhere. . . . "

I stare straight ahead. I keep driving and I try being quiet like Sissy. I don't say a word.

Sissy keeps looking back, but me—I have to face forward, look ahead, and pay attention to all the traffic signals. I don't need any more tickets.

"Martha's waiting for us," I finally say, but Sissy doesn't respond.

The rest of the ride, Sissy stays her usual no-talking self. But I can hear her thinking, and she's thinking real loud. She's thinking we'd better hurry so she's not late for her party. She's thinking about that little plastic mama in her bag and how Martha doesn't have any fancy paper to wrap it. Sissy's thinking about how lucky we are to get out of that no-parking-in-the-handicapped-zone citation, because Martha would've been mad for sure if I'd gotten another ticket. And Sissy's probably thinking about how she can blackmail me however she wants.

"You're not going to mention anything to Martha?" I say. "Right, Little Sister?"

Sissy gives me her sideways look.

"'Cause there's no need to say anything about the van, or which store we went to, or the cop and the handicapped zone, or the free ride I gave to that bag lady—I mean, the lady with the bags. Martha's got a lot on her mind. No need for you to worry her."

Sissy rolls up the edge of her bag and squeezes it tight like that plastic mama might try to jump out and run away. We're almost back to Martha's place.

"You wouldn't want to get your big brother in trouble now, would you? We got to look out for each other."

We turn onto our street. Sissy reaches over and sets the radio back to Martha's oldies station. I don't know why Martha likes all those old songs. I pull up to park. Martha's always complimenting me on my natural talent for parallel parking. She's right about that.

"So we understand each other, right?" I say to Sissy.

Sissy's not talking.

It's not till we're opening the front door and Martha's standing right there, holding the baby and saying "hi," that Sissy turns and whispers to me, "We're going back."

CHAPTER 4

That's downright tricky of Sissy. I can't argue with her in front of Martha, and Sissy knows it.

Martha blocks the door. She sees Sissy's Toy Mart bag and gives us an odd look, but she doesn't ask how we got there or what took us so long. Instead, Martha talks too loud in a fake friendly voice.

"Soli, Sissy, come say hello to Ms. Lupano, your new social worker. She's filling in while Karen is having a baby. Isn't that nice?"

The social worker in Martha's living room is younger than some of the other ones. I'm not shaking her hand.

"Hi," is all I say.

Ms. Social Worker ignores me and says hello to Sissy instead.

Then to Martha she says, "I was only assigned the girl's case, but my supervisor insisted I take all three."

"That's very kind of you to look after their best interests," Martha says.

Martha settles herself on the couch with the baby. He's fussing and scrunching up his face. Sissy stands near Martha.

"Aren't you going to say hello?" Martha prompts her.

"Hi," Sissy says, still clutching her bag.

"What's in the bag?" the lady asks.

"A mama," Sissy says, then she runs to her room. Sissy's got the right idea.

"Is something wrong with her?" the lady asks. She opens one of her files and clicks her pen.

"Sissy's cautious around strangers," Martha says. "But she's doing better every day. Don't you think, Soli?"

"Yeah, I guess so."

The social worker better stop clicking her pen. She reminds me of that jerk probation officer at juvie.

She's still clicking, and she acts like I don't even exist. "How did they get to the store?" she asks Martha. "And why didn't you go with them?"

"I was giving the baby his morning bath," Martha says. "Soli is very responsible. He's like a big brother to Sissy." She doesn't say anything about her knee hurting too much to take us anywhere—walking *or* driving. Martha checks her watch and says, "I better feed the baby. It's time for his bottle. It was nice of you to drop in, Shelly. May I call you Shelly?"

"It's Sheila—not Shelly, and both children need to be supervised at all times." Sheila-not-Shelly opens her big binder and starts flipping through it.

Martha stands up and switches the baby from one arm to the other. "How long will you be filling in for Karen? And did you have a chance to talk to her before her maternity leave—how's she doing?"

"Fine," says Sheila. "But Karen left the most disorganized office I've ever seen. I'm still trying to review everyone's files. Unlike Karen, I follow the rules."

Whoa, Sheila sounds like she needs a vacation. No rush catching up on my file, lady. I prefer Martha stays unclear on exactly how old I am. But I'd like to see my own file, find out what happened to my parents and how I got stuck in foster care. No one's ever told me that. I pieced together some stuff, but there's a lot I don't know.

"We appreciate what you're doing," Martha tells her. "I am sure you have a lot of children to keep track of."

"Yes," says Sheila. "I've got cases in San Francisco, Contra Costa,

Sonoma, and Napa counties. And now that Karen's out on maternity leave, my supervisor expects me to oversee her caseload too."

Martha walks to the door. Sheila closes her fat binder full of stupid rules and follows her.

"I won't keep you then," Martha says. "Thanks for stopping in. I bet you don't even have time for lunch with all those cases you're juggling. Give me a call next time, and I'll bake my macaroni and cheese."

"No thanks," Sheila says. "Visits are unannounced for a reason. And Toy Mart is far from here. How did they get to the store?"

"Soli knows all the bus lines," Martha says. Martha is good at stretching the truth without exactly lying. I admire that in a person.

"Look, Martha, the foster children in your care are to be supervised by an adult at all times." Sheila's voice is getting a tense edge to it again, like someone pulled her ponytail too tight.

Martha's swaying a bit. I don't know if she's rocking the baby or what.

"Our neighbor, Mrs. Morrow, gave us a ride to the store," I say. "We were supervised just fine."

Sheila opens a file and writes something down. She's still acting like I'm not even there.

"Does Mrs. Morrow have the required clearance from the Department of Social Services?"

"Uh-huh," Martha says. "I'm pretty sure Karen took care of that before she took her leave."

"I see." Sheila writes something down and gives her pen another click.

Martha's got the front door open. She smiles, puts her body at an angle, and then moves in slightly until Sheila is nudged out the door. Martha holds the baby so there's no room for the social worker to weasel herself back in.

Martha waves the baby's hand. "Bye-bye. Say 'bye-bye' to the nice lady," she says.

Sheila-not-Shelly does not wave back.

CHAPTER 5

I'm relieved she's gone, but I'm worried about that social worker's rule book, full of who knows what. I turn around and bump into Sissy.

"Was that a bad lady, or a good one?" Sissy asks.

"Probably a bad one," I say. I don't want to worry her, but the sooner she learns not to trust people, the better.

"Like the big bad wolf bad?" Sissy asks. Martha can't read her that "huff and puff and blow your house down" book anymore. It scared Sissy so much that Martha had to hide it.

"No. She's more like that other wolf. The one dressed up in Granny's clothes," I say. "She might look okay on the outside, but you got to be careful just the same."

Sissy nods.

Martha pours me a glass of milk while Sissy gets dressed for her party.

"That Sheila is a caseload all by herself," Martha says. "I've seen her kind before. Fresh out of college and on some kind of misguided crusade. Meanwhile she's got no sense of what's right. Always finding fault and never seeing the good."

Martha sips her ginger ale. Then she asks me, "Don't you think Sissy's starting to come out of her shell?"

I don't say anything but I think about it.

Martha's right.

I remember when Sissy first arrived at Martha's place. She was afraid of everything, and not just the big bad wolf story. She never said more than three words at a time, never smiled, never looked you in the eye, and she acted like she expected to be smacked any minute. One night after Sissy and the baby were asleep, Martha told me what happened to Sissy and why she never takes her sweater off. She's always pulling her sleeves down to cover the scars on her arms. Poor kid. I see why Sissy's so nervous and flinching. Why would anyone hurt a little kid like that? I've been punched and pushed around by other kids in the system. And by some adults. But nothing like what happened to Sissy.

About a month after she arrived at Martha's, Sissy started to relax. We were all unloading groceries in the kitchen one day and Martha had her oldies station blasting with that catchy "Hit the Road, Jack" song—even I liked it.

Martha was singing off tune real loud. I admit I was singing along, and banging the milk cartons to the beat, putting them into the fridge. Then I turned and saw Sissy all pale and quiet.

"What?" I asked.

Sissy wouldn't say. But she looked like she was stuck in a bad dream.

"Martha," I said, and I turned that music down quick.

Martha pulled Sissy onto her lap in the big old overstuffed rocking chair. Martha rocked her and said, "Something's bothering you, I know. You tell Martha, and you'll feel better. You're safe here."

Sissy let herself get rocked. She twisted the end of her braid around one finger, lost in some bad place all her own.

"That music bother you?" Martha asked.

Sissy nodded.

"Did we have it on too loud?"

Sissy shook her head no.

Martha took all the time in the world, humming some old church song I think I know but can't remember from where or when. She was rocking her and rocking her. I couldn't stand to watch so I put away the rest of the groceries, listening to Martha's humming. Humming down low like it was coming right out of Martha's heart. My throat got tight, and I tried to remember. Anyone ever rock me like that?

Finally Sissy looked like she was coming back to the real world, saying, "That Jack kid must be real bad. . . ."

"Hmmm?" said Martha.

"Jack's mama said he can't come back no more, ever. . . ."

Then Martha was hugging her tight, rocking and explaining. "Oh no, Sissy. Jack is not a child. That's all grownups' problems they're singing about. That woman is mad at her boyfriend. She doesn't even have any kids. Jack's a grown-up man, so he can take care of himself. No, we don't send children out on the road. Don't you worry about Jack."

"His mama don't want him," Sissy said.

That was Sissy a few months ago. Sissy's different now.

Yeah, Sissy's different. She's nervous about her friend's birthday party, and I'm nervous she's gonna tell Martha about me taking the van and giving a ride to that homeless lady—even though nothing bad happened. But I'm most nervous about Sissy whispering, "We're going back."

I have to set her straight about that.

Martha wants me to drive us all to the birthday party in case Sheila-not-Shelly is lurking around. Martha thinks that baby will stop fussing if he gets a ride in the van. He had his bottle of milk but he's still not happy. Actually he never looks too happy.

Martha packs up the baby as Sissy watches me out of the corner of her eye. I don't know if she's thinking about the old bag lady or the social worker. And I don't have a chance find out because Martha's right there.

I drive us to Sissy's friend's house, all painted bright yellow and white with gold trim. Martha's got to say hello to the birthday girl's mama so she limps up the stairs with Sissy, stopping halfway up to rub her bad knee. They look like they got a real nice house, but I'm just guessing because I have to stay in the van with the baby. He looks a little calmer now. He's just sitting in his baby seat behind me, so I slide on back to keep him company. He's not asleep, but he's not completely awake either. He's sitting there blinking his eyes—kind of wrinkle faced with his funny-shaped baby head.

"What's up, buddy?" I say. I use my soft voice so I don't startle him.

He's looking all around, but he can't quite figure out where I'm at.

"Yo, I'm over here. You think Sissy's gonna get me in trouble?"

That baby gets all jittery and he scrunches his little fists like he's mad at the world.

"I don't blame you, buddy."

He's working up to a full-blown crying fit. First his body shakes, and then he cries his pitiful cry. It's kind of screechy but not loud. Like he doesn't have enough air in his lungs or enough energy to be loud. Like he knows nobody's listening whether he's crying or not.

I'm listening. I jiggle the car seat and squeak his fuzzy duckie toy to try and calm him down.

"Hey now, don't get yourself all agitated. Life's not fair, but you got a chance. I'll be honest with you, it's not a very big chance. You got a little tiny scrawny chance—just your size."

Martha comes back, which is good, because it makes me nervous when that screechy baby gets himself worked up. I slide into the driver's seat, and Martha situates herself in the back. She sings a little *shush, shush* song while she tucks his blanket around his arms to calm him down.

"I see you and Baby Thaddeus were having a little chat," Martha says.

"It's a crime calling him that name. I bet they put his mother in jail for naming him that."

"His mama's not in jail. She's in rehab. And according to foster rules, that's what we're supposed to call him—so he knows who he is. Though I agree with you. Thaddeus doesn't exactly roll off your tongue. What do you think we should call him?" Martha asks.

I start up the engine, release the emergency brake, and ease away from the curb. I look at the baby in the rearview mirror and I think up all kinds of names, but I don't say them out loud. Crack Baby, Hopeless, Shaky Boy, Scrawny—yeah, Scrawny seems like a good name. Or maybe Pitiful. No chance in this world for a kid named Thaddeus or Scrawny or Pitiful.

"Chance," I say. "We should call him Chance."

"Chance," Martha says. "What do you say, Chance? You like it, hmm?"

That scrawny baby actually stops crying.

"But when the social worker comes 'round," Martha says, "his name is still Thaddeus, you hear?"

CHAPTER 6

A couple of hours later Martha and Chance are both sleeping. Martha doesn't usually take a nap.

"Martha, you want me to get Sissy?"

"Thanks," Martha says, half-asleep. "Look in my wallet for bus fare. You know where they live, right?"

"Yeah."

"Be careful, Soli. Sissy's friend Darlene and her mother are okay, but Darlene's father is an odd one. So do your best to make a good impression, okay?"

"Yeah."

I'll do my best all right. I'll do my best to make Sissy forget her crazy idea of us going back to find that old bag lady.

I wait until Martha is snoozing again, then I grab the keys to the van so we can stop at the auto supply store to look at the radar detectors on the way back. When I get to Darlene's house, the party's over. Everyone but Sissy has gone home. And Martha was right. Darlene's daddy is looking me over like I just burglarized his neighbors. Even as Sissy and I walk down the steps, he watches me from behind the curtains.

"How was the party?" I ask as I start the van.

Sissy clicks her seat belt and says, "Best birthday party I ever been to."

It's probably the only birthday party she's ever been to, but I don't say so.

"Did they have a big chocolate cake and ice cream?" I ask.

"No, they had pink cake with strawberry ice cream inside," Sissy says. "With frosting flowers and a mermaid on top. And they gave us all goody bags and little prizes—look!"

"Um-hmm," I say. "So you had a good time then?"

"Yes. Darlene has a mama and a daddy and a grandma, and a bunch of cousins, and she got so many presents—you can't believe how many presents she got. And Darlene has a pink bed like a princess sleeps there, with a lacy thing on top. And a dollhouse with so many rooms it looks like a castle. She let me play with it. I put the new mama from the toy store in there, and some brothers and sisters, and I moved 'em around all the rooms."

Sissy's talking so fast and stringing so many words together that she doesn't sound like Sissy at all. She sounds like Wired back at my last group home in Daly City after he'd downed too many Frappuccinos. They never should've put him in that work program at Starbucks.

"Did Darlene's mama give you coffee?" I ask.

"No," says Sissy. "But we had chocolate milk and pink milk and red juice—all we wanted. And a big bowl of jelly beans—all we wanted before the cake, and after the cake too. Look, I got some jelly beans in my goody bag. Pink and purple and red ones."

All those jelly beans and pink things at Darlene's party make Sissy forget all about the raggedy old bag lady. That's fine with me. I let her blabber on while I head to the auto-supply store.

I turn the radio up and Sissy's still talking away. We drive a few blocks. Then I notice Sissy's all silent.

"Now what?" I ask.

"Stop," she says.

If she wants to go looking for that bag lady, I'm not stopping.

"I feel si—" Sissy covers her mouth.

I slow down and Sissy tries to open her window, but she's not fast enough. When she throws up, that pink puke gets all over the inside of the window, all down the car door, onto her seat belt, all over Sissy, and even into her goody bag full of jelly beans.

I can forget about seeing that radar detector now. I turn us around, drive back to Martha's, and roll down my window for some fresh air. Sissy goes back to her usual no-talking self.

When we get back, I tell Martha that Darlene's folks called to say Sissy wasn't feeling so good and that's why I drove to get her. Martha gives Sissy a bath. She reads her that running away bunny book and makes her some chamomile tea.

And me? Martha gives me her yellow rubber gloves and says I have to clean the stinky pink puke out of the van.

"And no more taking the van out on your own," Martha says.

CHAPTER 7

Next morning Martha wakes me up and says we got to go to the clinic, and do I mind driving? I figure Sissy is still sick from all those birthday jelly beans, but Sissy's fine. It's Chance who's got a fever.

Even though I cleaned the van it still smells like day-old birthday barf.

"We'll shake some baking soda on it when we get back," Martha says. It smells so bad I'm feeling sick myself. I'm not waiting around in the stinky van, so I'm stuck looking after Sissy in the kids' waiting room while Martha takes Chance in to see the doctor.

Martha tells me, "Don't forget your workshop homework."

Martha signed me up for a Summer Teen Job Workshop without even asking me. It starts Thursday morning. There goes my laying-low plan for the summer, though I wouldn't mind making some money so I can buy my own car or a car stereo or that radar detector. Plus, I spent the last of my money on that bus zone burrito. And I still owe Martha two hundred and seventy-five bucks for the ticket.

I'm in the waiting room, flipping through my favorite car magazine—the issue with the customized vans—but Sissy keeps interrupting. She wants to tear some pictures out of the old magazines on the table. Ever since Darlene's party, she's got big plans to make a doll family—out of magazine pages. But she's afraid she'll get in trouble.

"Go ahead," I say. As long as she doesn't tear up the *Car & Truck* magazine Larry gave me when I left the Three Stooges group home, I don't care what she does.

Sissy shakes her head.

"No one cares about those junky magazines," I say. "Look how old they are."

"We got to go and ask," Sissy says. I know what that means—*I've got to go and ask.*

"Just show me the picture you want and I'll tear it out," I say.

Sissy shakes her head. So I take Sissy and the magazine up to the counter.

"Yes?" asks the lady.

"Sissy here wants permission to tear a page or two out of these old magazines. For her school project."

"Sure, dear," the lady says directly to Sissy. "You go right ahead."

Sissy walks back to the low table, whispering to me, "You lied, Soli. It's not for a school project."

"You want the pictures or not?"

Sissy grabs a magazine, sits on the floor, and gets busy. But she hands me the pictures to hold after she's torn them out. She acts like we're gonna be carted off to prison.

"Hide them in the back of your magazine," Sissy says.

I hardly have time to fill in any of the pages of my summer job homework, let alone read my *Car & Truck* magazine.

Martha finds us in the waiting room.

Sissy jumps up and rubs the baby's foot. "Is he okay?" she asks.

"He's gonna be fine. But he needs one more blood test. I have to walk him over to the lab. You done with your homework?" she asks me.

"I'm working on it." I show her my list with "Cars" written on the top. Underneath I wrote: *race car driver, mechanic, car salesman, delivery, taxi driver.*

"Good," Martha says. "You keep working on that and keep an eye on Sissy, okay?"

32

Sissy makes me read my list of car jobs aloud, like it's a bedtime story. Then I fold my homework pages and stick them in my magazine.

Sissy's torn out all the people from the first magazine and is looking around for more. I'm not letting her touch my magazine. We wait there forever. A lady sits down and starts blabbing away to me and Sissy about her new job.

"I'm finally gonna get paid what I'm worth. Plus lots of time off. Just one more test, and the final interview, then I'll be traveling all over the world. See that magazine there? I mingle with celebrities like that. You won't believe all the places I've been and the famous people I've met."

She's right. I don't believe her.

"Being a bodyguard nanny is the best job I've ever had."

"A bodyguard nanny?" Sissy says.

The lady snaps her gum and adjusts her ratty fur collar.

"Yeah," she says. "You know, like a nanny that takes care of kids. Like *Mary Poppins*. You seen that movie, hon?"

Sissy nods.

"So I'm just like Mary Poppins, only I'm a nanny for rich and famous people, and I'm their bodyguard too." She goes on and on about how she used to watch the kids of this and that movie star or sports celebrity but she can't tell us who because it's "top secret."

Yeah, right.

I open my magazine again and read the article about the guy who bought a cheap old van, tricked out the inside, and went camping all over the country, watching comets and falling stars through his custom-welded moonroof. Sissy listens to the lady brag about how she knows martial arts to protect rich kids in case someone tries to kidnap them from their expensive private schools.

"I know jujitsu," the lady says.

"Jujitsu?" Sissy asks.

"Yep," the lady says. "And you know, most of the families have their own chauffeur. He drives us all over town, wherever we need to go in a Rolls Royce."

"Do they have big houses with princess rooms?" Sissy asks.

"Of course," says Ms. Bodyguard-Nanny-of-the-Unnamed-Rich-and-Famous.

Judging by her short skirt, long painted fingernails, smelly perfume, and thick makeup, this lady has some other occupation. I pull my homework from the back of my magazine, unfold it, and try to write chauffeur on my job list. But it's a hard word to spell. *Shofer? Choufer? Chaufer?* None of them look right. So I write *driver for rich people* and leave it at that.

"I'm thirsty," the lady says. "I'm going to get a sip of water. You thirsty, hon?" she asks Sissy.

Sissy nods, then she looks at me. I can see the water fountain down the hall so I let her go. That nanny wannabe wouldn't get far in her rickety high heels.

Jujitsu? Right.

Sissy goes with her to the water fountain over and over again. She's so thirsty you'd think that nanny had eaten a bucket or two of salted peanuts. But at least she's keeping Sissy occupied so I can look at my magazine. It's full of expensive custom vehicles, and someday I'm going to get me some wheels like that. Maybe a big truck or camper. I could get away from California and every foster place I ever lived and see all those states I've never been to. I'll find Wired again and we can drive across the country like we planned. Wired wanted to go to Las Vegas. Me, I'd like to see the Grand Canyon or the car show in Reno.

Ms. Mary Poppins is telling Sissy about how she has diamonds embedded in her cell phone cover. It looks like fake glued-on plastic rhinestones to me. And if she's so rich, why are her shoes so scuffed and her clothes so ratty? But hey, I'm not questioning her career goals. Especially with Sissy so wide-eyed and not bothering me anymore. So I just keep reading the ads for cars and wondering when I can afford one of my own. The customized '63 Ford Deluxe Club Wagon with the built-in fridge, captain's chairs, and triple chrome-plated bumpers looks good.

Sissy is wiggling and says, "Soli, I gotta go pee."

"Wait for Martha," I say.

"I can't wait."

"You shouldn't have drunk so much water."

"I'll take you, hon," the lady says.

"I don't know," I say.

"Don't worry," the lady says. "We're not going far—the powder room is just beyond the water fountain."

I tell them to hurry up 'cause Martha's gonna be out soon, then I watch them head down the hall and around the corner. It's not like I can go into the ladies' bathroom or take Sissy into the men's room, so what choice do I have?

I try to read my *Car & Truck* magazine. I watch people going up and down the hallway, but Sissy and that wannabe nanny are taking too long. So I go down the hall, around the corner, and pace outside the first bathroom door I see. It's one of those unisex ones. I listen at the door. People are giving me strange looks. What? They think I'm going to break in and steal a toilet seat or something? The metal latch says "Occupied," but I check the door handle anyway.

Locked.

So I knock. Then I pound on the door.

"Sissy! Hurry up in there. What's taking you so long?"

I listen again and I finally hear a flush. About time.

But it's not Sissy. An old man opens the door. I push past him.

"Hey, young man!" he shouts—but no one else is in there.

I hurry down the hall and back around the corner. They're not back in the waiting room. I ask the lady behind the counter where the bathrooms are.

"The men's room is—"

"No," I say. "I'm looking for my little sister."

She points down another hall and I'm running.

"Sissy!"

I come to a ladies' room and I lean against the door so it creaks halfway open.

"Sissy, you in there?"

Nothing. I go in—but no one's there. I open each stall. Nobody. Men's room. Nobody.

I come to an elevator and the stairs. Could they have gone up?

I open a glass exit door to a side street and shout, "Sissy!"

They couldn't have left the building. Or could they? My gut tells me they didn't. So I stay on the same floor. Another turn in the hallway. Another women's restroom. I swing the door open and listen.

Muffled voices. Some kind of scuffling.

"No!" Sissy's shouting. "No, I don't want to."

CHAPTER 8

I race in there.

"Sissy!"

Sissy crawls out from under the stall near the door. The weird nanny sees me and steps closer to the sinks, hiding something behind her back.

"Soli," Sissy says, reaching for me. She grabs my hand tight and I pull her out. She scrambles to her feet and tugs at me. "Run, Soli! She knows jujitsu."

I push Sissy ahead of me and she runs out of the restroom. Scary Mary Poppins runs too. She pushes past me and runs the other way—down the hall, out the glass exit door, and down the sidewalk.

Sissy comes back and we watch that weird nanny wannabe. She's got her skirt hiked up and she's carrying her high heels. I want to chase after her and yell at her not to mess with Sissy or any other little kids. But she's faster than I ever expected. Fast and out of sight.

"Are you okay, Sissy?" I ask. I kneel down so I can see her face. I squeeze her skinny shoulders. "What happened?"

"She had a cup. And she wanted me to pee in it," Sissy says. "I didn't want to but she said I had to. I told her I needed my privacy. Then I locked the door so she couldn't get me."

"I shouldn't have let her take you. Did she . . . she didn't hurt you or anything?"

"No," Sissy says. "She wanted my pee. For a test—for her job. That's weird. So I locked my door and didn't come out."

"You were smart." I say.

"I know," Sissy says. "If I was a rich movie star I wouldn't hire her. Is she really a bodyguard nanny?"

"I don't think so."

"Me neither," Sissy says.

"You okay now?"

"Um-hmm. You scared her away, Soli. But why'd she want my pee?"

Scary Mary Poppins must have been doing drugs. That's why she wanted Sissy to pee in the cup. To pass a drug test.

"Rich people have weird tests," I say.

"Yeah," says Sissy. "They do."

Sissy brushes off her sweater and sticks her hands in her pockets. "Soli?" she says.

"Yeah?"

"I still have to go."

So I wait outside the door while Sissy goes back in.

"I'll be right here," I say.

I stand there thinking about all the bad stuff Martha told me happened to Sissy. She comes back out a few minutes later.

"Sissy, you sure you're okay?"

"Yeah," says Sissy. "But don't tell Martha because Martha told me not to go with strangers. And that lady was *strange*."

"Yeah," I say. "We don't have to tell Martha—because nothing really bad happened."

Sissy is quiet.

So I ask again. "Nothing really bad happened, right?"

"Right," Sissy says. "She just wanted my pee."

She starts walking back to the waiting room.

Sissy's not going to tell Martha. So why don't I feel relieved?

When we get back, Martha's holding Chance and looking for us.

"There you are," she says.

Sissy says, "I had to go pee," before Martha can ask a million questions.

"Thanks for watching Sissy," Martha says.

"Sure," I say, but it feels like I just swallowed a bunch of lug nuts and they're clunking around in the pit of my stomach.

After Martha picks up Chance's medicine, we all walk back to the van.

Sissy tells me, "Soli, you should write 'bodyguard' on your job list. You'd be a good one."

Now I feel worse.

CHAPTER 9

When we get back, Martha gives Chance his medicine. He looks like he's perking up. She hands me a big box of baking soda to sprinkle inside the stinky van.

"Go liberal," Martha tells me.

So I shake it all over. On the floor, on the seats—especially where Sissy was sitting. I try to make some stick to the window and on the inside of the door where she puked. It's not sticking—it just slides down to the floor. Martha said if we leave the baking soda for a day or two before we sweep it out, it'll take away the odor. I have my doubts, but anything would be better than how it smells right now.

The next day Sissy is cutting out more paper people and sticking them in a shoe box she calls their home. Martha's singing out of tune again along with the oldies on the radio. As usual she's getting half the lyrics wrong. I swear I hear her singing, "Sweet dreams are made of cheese," but maybe that's because she's fixing macaroni and cheese for lunch.

After lunch I bring in some boxes I find next to the neighbors' recycling bin.

I sit near Sissy with Martha's scissors and her roll of duct tape.

"You be careful with my poultry scissors," Martha says.

"Yeah," I say.

"What are you making?" Sissy asks.

"You'll see."

I cut out some doors and windows and Sissy knows right away what it's going to be. She's not smiling but she can barely sit still.

"It's a house," Sissy says. "Just like Darlene's. Look, Martha. Soli's making me a dollhouse."

"I see," Martha says. "Good idea, Soli."

I hand Sissy the door and window scraps. "If you glue your paper people onto these, they'll last longer."

"Thanks."

I tape the boxes together with Martha's duct tape and it looks pretty good. A house with four rooms. Sissy moves in her magazine people and gets busy cutting up more. She glues them onto cardboard scraps like I told her. Sissy likes the cardboard house so much that she forgets all about Scary Mary Poppins and the Toy Mart bag lady. That's fine with me. I don't need her telling Martha about those people, especially since nothing bad happened.

Sissy makes herself a doll family—a big, weird, paper-doll family full of movie stars, athletes, supermodels and their dogs. Sissy doesn't know who they are. She's playing with the president—moving him in and out of the house. And some rappers, and the Stanford women's basketball team, and some bearded guy in a white robe, and that boy genius—like they're one big happy family. She calls them Mama, Baby, Big Brother, the Cousins, Grandpa—names like that. Most of them are cut crooked, and she's using up all of Martha's Scotch tape so their cardboard heads don't flop down. I bet Sissy has more dolls now than Darlene.

I look at my homework again and Martha's got the radio on. Sissy still doesn't sing along with the songs. She's just playing with her cardboard dolls and talking quiet to herself. But when Martha puts Chance down for a nap, Sissy all of a sudden looks up from her magazine people. One minute she's cutting out hurricane victims and gluing an old lady in a wheelchair onto cardboard, saying, "This one looks like a grandma—" and the next minute? She remembers.

"We have to go find that lady," Sissy says.

"What lady?"

"You know who," Sissy says. "The lady at the toy store."

I pretend I have no idea what she's talking about.

"The one you gave a ride to," Sissy insists. "The grandma one we left in the rain."

"We'll never find her. I don't even remember where we let her off."

"Tenth Street," Sissy says, "and a street with a *B*."

"Why do you want to find that raggedy old lady?"

"We gotta check on her."

"Why?"

"Because we have to."

Sissy's hard to argue with. Back at the group home, I could talk my way out of a tight spot, swap chores, and convince those counselors and troublemaking kids of pretty much anything, just by switching their words around. That's why they started calling me Shifty. But now that I've been at Martha's a while, I'm out of practice. I look at skinny seven-year-old Sissy, with her brown eyes so intense. She's kind of scary, so I start talking without thinking.

"Even if we drive up and down Tenth Street looking for a street with a *B*—and there's a lot of streets with *B*s in them—then what? You think we're gonna find that old lady? You think she's gonna be sitting on her front porch waving to us as we cruise by?"

"Maybe," Sissy says.

"Then what? You think she's going to invite us in for a glass of lemonade? Is that what you think?"

Sissy's eyes well up. A big old tear rolls down one cheek. A big silent tear screaming how mean I am. She looks down the hall toward

42

Chance's room where Martha is.

Sissy stands up.

"Oh, no. You're not going to go crying to Martha about that old bag lady, are you?"

"Maybe," Sissy says. "And she's not a bag lady. She's a lady with bags. Maybe I'll tell Martha about the jujitsu nanny too."

"Sissy, wait a minute. Come back," I say. "Let's add some more rooms to your dollhouse."

But she's already walking down the hall toward Chance's door. And she's gonna tell Martha.

CHAPTER 10

I follow Sissy down the hall. The wooden rocking chair in Chance's room stops creaking and Martha comes out.

I can't say anything so I slowly shake my head at Sissy.

She ignores me. "Martha," Sissy says, "you still need diapers?"

"Thanks for reminding me. We are running low," Martha says, rubbing her knee. "I have a buy one get one free coupon for diapers at Toy Mart. Do you mind carrying back two jumbo packs of disposables on the Mission bus, Soli? And maybe you could refill my prescription at Rite Aid while you're at it. My knee's bothering me."

"I'm going too," Sissy says. "I can help carry the diapers."

"Okay, but hurry back," Martha says. "I'd hate to see that pushy social worker snooping around here, asking where you are."

Martha doesn't notice but Sissy grabs the keys to the van.

"Hurry, Soli," Sissy says, handing me the keys out front. "Quick, before Martha sees us."

Sissy brushes baking soda off her seat but we don't have time to sweep it all up. Besides, the van still smells. She makes me drive down Tenth Street, insisting we look for that old lady before we get the diapers. So I let her look. After a while she'll see it's hopeless. We'll get the diapers and still have time to go to the auto-supply store.

After we've been driving up and down Tenth Street for a while, I say, "Okay, this is Tenth and Brannan again. Anything look familiar?"

Sissy shakes her head.

"Tenth and Bryant. You see her anywhere?"

Sissy shoots me one of her looks. She's getting mad.

"You wanna go down Tenth Street again?" I ask.

She doesn't answer, so I drive to the toy store. We park in a legal spot and get the diapers. Sissy's still bent out of shape as we get back in the van and head to the auto-supply store. She's doing her silent thing.

"I'm not in charge of all the homeless people in San Francisco," I say.

"People with no homes," Sissy says.

I don't bother answering. I open my window and tilt my head so the breeze cools my face.

Sissy glares at me. "And you forgot Martha's medicine."

Now I'm ticked off. So when I see a paper bag in the middle of the intersection I run over it, just because I feel like running over something. I'm expecting a good loud lunch-bag-popping sound.

But as soon as I run over that bag—in the moment the van swerves and I realize that bag wasn't empty—I get a sinking feeling. I hear scraping metal under us, and I remember Larry back at the group home. He's in my brain along with the tire popping and the screeching brakes. Larry's saying, "Too bad you're not thinking things through, Soli. Too many mistakes and you're going to get the big X." I heard his stupid X story so many times.

I tighten my grip on the steering wheel and turn into the swerve. Good thing I studied Wired's driver's manual. Sissy's knuckles are squeezed tight—she's clutching her seat belt in one hand and the door handle in another.

The van stops at a crazy angle. It smells like burnt rubber, and my stomach feels like we're still turning.

"I'm gonna be sick," Sissy says.

"Oh no. No more throwing up."

This time she doesn't.

Of course there's no place to park. Cars are veering around us and

45

the nails scattered all over the intersection. They're honking like it's my fault. It's not my fault. I didn't put those nails in that paper bag. Why would anyone put a huge bag full of nails right in the middle of the street?

Some of the boys and me at the Three Stooges group home tossed little packets of takeout ketchup and mustard in the street to see them squish—but nothing like this.

I make Sissy wait on the sidewalk where she'll be safe. A lady with two dogs pulls out of a driveway. She says I can park there and check my tires. Looks like the left front tire is totally gone—shredded and falling off the rim. And there's a nail stuck straight into the left rear tire. Too bad we only have one spare.

Before I can even jack up the van, Sissy says, "You better go pick up those nails."

"What?"

"You gotta pick up all those nails," she says. "So no one else busts their tire."

"Are you crazy? You want me to get hit by a car like Martha and go around with an artificial leg? No way!"

But two minutes later I'm scooping up nails from the middle of the intersection as fast as I can. And Sissy? She's directing traffic. She should put "traffic cop" on *her* career list. When the light turns red one way, she stands in the crosswalk and holds up her hands to stop traffic. And the cars all stop, even though a couple of them honk at us. Then I'm running like crazy, scooping up nails until I can't pick up any more, because the ones in my pockets are jabbing into my legs. A street-sweeper guy sees me, sets up some orange cones, and helps with his broom. Cars stop honking and move along after that.

Sissy's back on the sidewalk watching me as I jack up the van and replace the worst flat tire with the spare. The other tire still has a nail in it, and I think I'll pull it out. But the sweeper guy says that if I leave it, I can drive a little longer. I stand there looking at the van, and it's tilting slightly to the left. We'll have to skip the auto-supply store and head back to Martha's. How am I going to explain two flat tires when I'm not even supposed to be driving her van?

Then a police car pulls up.

One cop gets out and walks over to our van as I put the jack away and close the back door.

"We got a call saying there was a disturbance at this intersection," he says.

Sissy eases away, climbs into the passenger seat, and shuts the door. Good idea.

"I haven't seen any disturbance," I say. I walk to the driver side, but the cop is right behind me.

"You don't know anything about juveniles blocking traffic and debris in the street?" he says.

Sissy watches and listens through my open window.

"Well, sir, we did have a little trouble, but we got it all cleared up now."

"What kind of trouble?"

"Someone dropped a bag of nails in the street and I accidentally ran over it."

I point to the flattened bag in the gutter, some nails near the curb, and I pull some more nails out of my pocket.

The cop is silent.

I showed him the proof. What more does he want? I pull out my keys and reach for the door.

The cop's still looking at me.

So I continue. "All I saw was a big paper bag."

"No one was blocking the flow of traffic?" he asks.

"No, we were redirecting it. My little sister, she was helping me on account of she was concerned about those nails. Right, Sissy? We got a flat and she didn't want anyone else to get a punctured tire. We thought it'd be a good idea to get all the nails out of the way. That city street sweeper helped—"

I look around, but the street-sweeper guy is gone.

The cop looks at me, then at Sissy. Sissy sinks lower in her seat, and pulls her sweater over her knees.

I have to get out of here before he asks to see my license. I open the car door, slide in behind the wheel, and pull the door shut. He's peering into the van. "What's that white powdery substance?"

"Baking soda," I say.

"I threw up," says Sissy.

"Baking soda makes the smell go away." I put the key in the ignition.

The cop sniffs the air and takes a step back like he doesn't want to get too close.

"Buckle your seat belt, Sissy."

"Wait," the cop says. "Don't move." Then he motions to his partner. "Officer Yeomans," he calls. "Can you come here a minute?"

The other cop is still in the police car talking on her radio. I can hear it through the open window. She gets out and walks over to us. That lady cop raises her sunglasses and looks right at Sissy and me. Sissy slinks even lower. It's the same cop from in front of the toy store—the cop that wanted to give me a ticket a couple of days ago for parking in the handicapped zone. And she recognizes me, I can tell.

I try to smile, keep quiet, and act like nothing's wrong.

"It's you," she says. "I've been looking for you."

CHAPTER 11

Me?"

I'm surprised the cops don't hear my heart thumping.

"Yes," the lady cop says. "I'm glad we ran into you. We couldn't find any ID on her. No phone numbers or anything, and after your grandma's seizure, she couldn't remember much."

"My grandma?"

The cop opens a little spiral notepad.

"Yes. Your grandma is named Ann or Annie, right? She told us her last name was Simmons, or Simpson?"

I don't know what to say so I just nod.

"We responded to a call about an hour ago from the shopping center where I saw you a few days ago. She had some kind of seizure in the Jamba Juice. The ambulance took her to S.F. General. I'll radio ahead and tell the hospital you're coming. I know this must be a shock."

"Yeah," I say. "It's a real shock."

Next thing I know we're driving on a tilt, with the tires going *whumpata-whumpata* and the cops right behind us all the way to San Francisco General.

We pull into the hospital parking garage. The cops wave and drive off. I'm ready to drive right back out but Sissy has other ideas.

"We're already here," she says.

"This hospital's huge. Look at all the buildings," I say. "How we gonna find her?"

"Her name's Annie Simmons . . . or Simpson," Sissy says.

"Martha's gonna be worried. We're late already. She told us to come right back."

"Call Martha and tell her we got a flat tire."

"Martha told us to take the bus, remember?"

"I forgot," says Sissy. "Look, a parking spot."

"Oh no," I say. "I'm not parking in a handicapped space."

I finally park legally and find a phone to call Martha. I tell her the buses are running slow. I don't say anything about taking her van, or the nails and the cops, or that we're at S.F. General looking for our fake grandma. Best to keep the story simple.

Sissy goes with me to the information desk. She almost smiles when we find out Annie is in room 308. I don't feel good about this. Last time Sissy was almost smiling, I had to clean up all that stinky pink puke.

"We'll say Annie is our grandma," Sissy says. "Gramma Annie."

Gramma Annie. Right. I don't like the way the hallway smells. I don't like the pale blue uniforms and white smocks everybody's wearing. Or the way their shoes squeak. I don't like the way the elevator door lurches open and shut. Makes my stomach lurch too.

Sissy pushes the button for the third floor.

"What are we going to say?" I ask.

"We can say hi." The doors rattle open and she proceeds down the hall to room 308.

A nurse walks out as we walk in. "Sorry," she says. "Regular visiting hours are over. Immediate family only now."

"But she's our grandma," Sissy says.

The nurse squints at us and checks her chart. "Really? Okay, I'll be back."

The old lady sits up, stares at Sissy, then at me. She's got a bandage on her forehead and an IV dripping into her. What are we doing here?

"How you feeling?" says Sissy.

"Woozy. This lemonade helps. You want some?"

She holds up a yellow juice box in her shaky, wrinkled hand. Sissy's eyes get big but she says, "No thanks."

It gives me the creeps. The little straw in the juice box looks like one of the tubes going into the old lady's arm.

"I gotta get out of here," Annie says.

Me too.

"I need to get home to Lester," the old lady says. "Who are you? You're not my family."

I back up toward the door, but Sissy, she's brave. She moves closer to that strange lady's bed.

"We gave you a ride that rainy day. Remember?" Sissy says.

"I remember. Hand me my paper bag in the closet over there. Lester is going to be worried."

"You want us to call Lester and tell him where you are?" I ask. "Then Lester can come check on you, 'cause we gotta be going."

"Don't be ridiculous," she says. "We haven't had a phone in years. You have to go there and tell him."

She writes down an address on Harrison Street. "We're in unit twenty-seven. Here's the key," she says. "He's gonna be hungry, but I got his favorite dinner in the bag. You give him some of that and tell him I'll be home tomorrow. You do that, okay?"

"Okay," Sissy says, before I can stop her.

And that's not the worst part. When we get in the elevator and look in the bag at Lester's dinner, it's a small bottle of water and a big can of cat food.

"Sissy, this is crazy. We can't do this."

"Why not?"

"Because either Lester is a cat, or he's a strange guy who eats cat food."

"Either way," Sissy says, "Lester's hungry."

CHAPTER 12

We're driving down Harrison Street and Martha's van is still on a slight tilt from the spare tire. Sissy grips that old lady's key and address in her hands so tight that the paper's getting all wrinkled.

We cross Tenth Street onto Bryant.

"See?" Sissy says. "Annie lives near a street with a *B*."

"Uh-huh."

If Lester's a man, we'll just hand him his food and the key. I'll tell him Annie's at the hospital. Then he and the old lady can take care of themselves—and we'll be on our way.

"If it doesn't look safe," I warn Sissy, "you're not getting out of the van. And I decide if it looks safe. Not you." I double-check the automatic door lock, and Sissy cuts me a look. I slow down, expecting to find a big old dumpy apartment building. Maybe a residence hotel or motel.

But it's not like that at all.

"Let me see that address again," I say.

She hands me the paper. That's the address all right.

"Sissy," I say. "This is a storage place. People don't live here."

"Annie lives here, and so does Lester," she says. "Where's twenty-seven?"

We drive up and down the rows until we get to the unit with "27" painted in red on the front. Lester better be a cat. Because what kind of person would live in a storage unit?

I look up and down the alley. No one's in sight. I shift into park, turn off the engine, and set the brake.

I'm thinking about Larry's X story again.

"Come on," says Sissy. She opens her door, grabs the paper bag, and jumps down.

The door to twenty-seven is like one of those roll-up garage doors. Sissy hands me the key and I'm hoping it won't fit the lock. But it does.

"Should we knock to tell Lester we're here?" Sissy asks.

Good idea. Just in case Lester-the-Cat is not Lester-the-Cat. Just in case he is Lester-the-Big-Hungry-Maniac. But why would that old lady lock up a person inside a storage unit? He's got to be cat—not that I like cats much either. Sissy's squeezing that bag so tight you can see the outline of the water bottle and the can of cat food right through the brown paper. I've heard about some people so poor they had to eat cat food.

I look down the alley again to make sure no one is coming, and right then Sissy bangs on the metal door, rattling my insides.

"What'd you do that for?" I say.

"You're supposed to knock."

"You ready?" I say, sliding the lock off. "If Lester threatens you, run back to the van as fast as you can. And lock your door."

Sissy nods all serious, like she's been breaking into strange people's storage units for years.

"We got your dinner, Lester," Sissy calls. "Annie sent us."

I squat down and roll up the door a couple of feet. I hate that metal-against-metal sound.

Sissy is right there beside me, then she's under the door, disappearing into the dark. I can't see a thing.

"Sissy, get back here!"

I squeeze past a wall of stacked boxes. It smells like a pet store.

"I can't reach it," Sissy says.

My eyes adjust and Sissy's stretching for a little chain next to a bare lightbulb. An extension cord's hanging from the same socket. I pull the chain and the light goes on, sending our shadows swaying across the room. Feels like this room is filled with ghosts. Does that lady actually live in here? And where's Lester? At least no crazy maniac is after us.

Yet.

We walk across a worn-out red carpet with fringed edges and fancy black swirls. The carpet looks like it belongs in a nice house, not in a cold, stinky, cinder-block storage room with no windows and a metal roll-up door. But it feels right, too, like we're in someone's living room. Like the carpet's been there for years and years under that green flowered sofa chair. There's a low table and a bookcase filled with books and junk. I keep looking around for Lester, but there's nobody here besides Sissy and me. It smells bad but it's still a nicer setup than some of the foster places I've lived in.

A hot plate and a toaster oven are plugged into an extension cord going up to the light socket. My shop teacher would say the outlet is dangerously overloaded.

I wonder what it costs to rent a place like this.

Sissy stares wide-eyed at everything. Her mouth is slightly open and she keeps reaching to touch things—a framed photo of a man in a uniform, a ball of yarn, and some old glass bottles—but she pulls her hand back just before making contact.

Cardboard boxes line the back wall. Four tires—rims and all—are stacked in the corner with a green pillow on top. I move the pillow over to some boxes and look at the tires. They have good treads, and the rubber smells better than anything else in the room. I try to read the numbers on the top tire to see if they're the right size. I lean in closer, hoping the bolt pattern matches Martha's van—that's when he jumps out at me.

"Whoa!" I stumble back.

The biggest, scariest cat I've ever seen lands on the pillow right next to me. I don't like cats—especially huge, scary ones leaping out of the dark. He looks mean, like he's gonna attack. That big orange beast twitches his striped tail back and forth, staring me down.

"Lester?" Sissy says. "Are you Lester?"

"*Meowp*," says the cat.

I never had a pet and I never wanted one. But Sissy comes close to that strange cat like she knows what she's doing. She's crazy brave. She puts her hand out real slow for the cat to sniff.

"Careful, Little Sister. That cat's ferocious. He'll scratch you. Or bite you. And I bet he's got rabies."

But that fat furry cat is the first thing Sissy touches in the old lady's room. She touches his head and rubs between his ears. She pets his striped back while the cat stretches his neck down low and holds his tail end up in the air. When she rubs under his chin, that cat lets out a loud rumbling purr. He's pumping his paws up and down on the pillow—the one that's sitting on top of those boxes next to the tires I want. And I can't tell who's liking it more—that gigantic orange cat—or Sissy.

"Hey Lester, you hungry?" she says. Sissy picks up that hunk of a cat and sits herself down in the green flowered chair. Lester walks in a circle on her lap, then plops himself down, sniffing at her sweater and pushing his big head against her hand.

I look for the can opener while Sissy bosses me around. She makes me close the metal door so the cat can't escape. She's acting like the Queen of Sheba, worried about King Lester the Cat.

"Hurry up, Soli," she tells me. "Don't worry, Lester—we'll feed you."

"*Meowp*," says the cat. That cat is weird. He can't even meow right.

It's such a small room, you'd think it'd be easy to find a can opener, but that old lady has everything in odd places. She's got maple syrup next to postage stamps, balls of yarn in an old ice chest, pajamas and other clothes in a box next to the tires. But no can opener.

"It's all right, Lester," Sissy says, petting the cat some more. "Gramma Annie will be back tomorrow."

She stops talking and watches me. "Look in the ice chest again," she says. Real helpful, Sissy is.

I finally find a can opener behind a box of coupons and paper scraps. It's an ancient one from who knows when. I can't figure out how to hook it onto the can.

"Let me see," Sissy says. She turns the can over. "Look, there's a pop-top." She hands it back to me.

I pop the can open and that creepy lump of a cat leaps off Sissy's lap. He rubs up against my legs, singing his loud *meowp* song. I let him eat right out of the can because I can't find another cat bowl other than his water dish, and I don't want to touch that smelly stuff any more than I have to. Good thing Lester is a cat, because no human should have to eat that slime.

Sissy looks for a bag to empty the stinky litter box. But she freezes when someone bangs on the metal door yelling, "Who's in there?"

CHAPTER 13

Sissy grabs the giant cat and carries him behind a wall of boxes in the back. She's gone in a flash. Where'd she learn to hide so fast? Me, I can't move that quick. But I can think fast. I pull down the top tire from the stack, check to make sure Sissy is hidden, then lift the metal door. I roll the tire out past the box barricade, into the sunshine, squinting at the beer-bellied whiskery guy sitting on his three-wheeled motorized cart.

"Hello," I say, pulling the door back down. He looks like he's some kind of oversized, rough-tough cowboy sheriff, ready to haul me in. I look up and down the alley. At least he doesn't have a posse.

"What are you doing in there?" he says. He's got bushy eyebrows, gray stubble covering his double chin, and wiry gray hairs growing out of his nose and ears.

"Just getting a tire. Fixing my flat," I say.

He can't argue with that. The tire with the nail in it is even lower than before.

I whistle one of Martha's old songs while I pull out the jack and start jacking the van up. He takes off his baseball cap, rubs his oily hair, then puts his cap back on. He's watching me. I keep whistling and working on the tire.

I have to smile to myself because I'm whistling the, "Don't It Make My Brown Eyes Blue" song I heard Martha singing along with the radio this morning. Except Martha was singing, "Donuts make my brown eyes blue."

Mr. Three-Wheeler's got fierce blue-gray eyes and he looks like he's had more than a few donuts himself. He finally says, "Gotta keep my eyes open for any undesirable element around here. If you see anyone suspicious, let me know. You can find me down at the office or patrolling in the security vehicle here." He pats the cart like it's his trusty horse.

"Okay," I say, and he tools off in that dinky three-wheeler, putt-putting at five miles an hour.

If Wired was here, he'd call that guy an Old Fart, and we'd both be laughing at his cart and the fart noises coming from it. Wired would be scheming how to get back here late at night to hot-wire that three-wheeler for a not-too-speedy joyride.

I have to call Larry to see if he knows where Wired is.

The security guy is gone, and the first tire is replaced. So I lift the door, roll our old tire in, and grab a new one from the stack.

"He's gone," I say.

Sissy comes out of hiding, still holding the cat.

"We have to go as soon as I replace the other tire," I say.

"We can't leave Lester."

"Oh yes we can. We're not taking that stinky cat with us."

Sissy holds that cat tight. "Lester's not stinky. It's his litter box. Let's take him to Martha's."

"No, we're leaving him here. Besides, he'd probably run away from Martha's, and then Annie would be mad at you. You wouldn't want that, would you?"

I change the other tire while Sissy empties the litter box. I stack the two bad tires on top of Annie's two good ones and I put Lester's pillow back on top. Sissy leaves Lester on the big chair and pets his head. Then she fills his litter box with torn newspaper. Lester's watching everything she does. Me too.

"You had a cat before?" I ask.

"No," Sissy says. "But my teacher said I was the best pet helper in Room Twelve. I took care of Oprah."

"Oprah?"

"Room Twelve's hamster," Sissy says. "You want to know why they named her Oprah?"

"Why?"

"Because everyone loves watching her."

Sissy's serious—she doesn't even know she's telling a joke. No smile—nothing.

"Okay, Sissy. We gotta go."

"Bye, Lester," Sissy says, her forehead right up close to his. She turns to me. "Lester wants to come with us."

"He can't. We'll check on him in a couple of days," I say.

"Tomorrow," she says.

"Fine."

"Don't worry, Lester. We'll be back," Sissy tells the cat, as if he understands English.

"*Meowp.*"

Sissy follows me outside, still talking to the cat as I pull the scraping metal door down and attach the lock.

"*Meowp,*" Lester says from inside. It reminds me of Chance's pitiful cry, far away and like no one is listening.

CHAPTER 14

We head for the exit on Harrison Street but the Old Fart is sitting on his three-wheeler, blocking the road. I slow down. Sissy slouches as low as she can go.

"Sit up," I tell her. "Don't look so guilty. There's no way he can prove the tires are stolen."

"He looks mad." Sissy sits up a little and brushes baking soda off the seat.

"Don't say anything," I whisper. "Let me do the talking."

I slow to a stop, roll down the window, and wave at the Old Fart, as if he's not blocking the only exit out of this place like a police barricade on a TV cop show.

"What's up?" I ask, all friendly.

"Who said you could enter unit twenty-seven?"

"Our Aunt Annie," I say. "She said I could use her tires—and she wanted us to check on her stuff—make sure it was safe."

Sissy nods her head.

"Where is she?" the Old Fart asks.

"She's, uh, resting up at . . . at . . ."

"At a mud spa," Sissy says, leaning toward my window. "They give you baths in hot mud and it makes you feel young. And they have hot bubbly water that comes right out of the ground that way. Families go in the hot water together—kids too—but only the grown-ups are allowed in the mud. And they put cucumbers on your eyes to cool you down."

I can't believe Sissy's talking about hot mud and cucumbers, but the good thing is the Old Fart can't get a word in. He looks like someone let the air out of his tires.

"Annie likes mud baths," Sissy says.

Then Sissy takes a breath, leans back, and twists her braid.

She's done talking. Completely. I don't know what to say.

The Old Fart starts up again. "You tell your aunt I checked our records and her rent is past due. If she's got enough money to sit her rear in fancy mud, she's got enough to pay her rent. If she doesn't pay, we'll saw off the lock and auction off her belongings."

I don't want to know but I ask anyway. "How much does she owe?"

"One hundred and ninety-six bucks. And it was due last week. She's got till the day after tomorrow, then we're selling her stuff."

"I'll remind her," I say.

The Old Fart adjusts his baseball cap and rolls his three-wheeler out of the way. We drive out of there and I look at Sissy.

"Mud baths and cucumbers?" I say.

Sissy shrugs.

"Where'd you hear that?"

"Darlene showed me her mama's spa magazine."

We haven't driven more than two blocks when Sissy says, "We got to go back and get Lester."

"That Old Fart will be watching. If we go back now, we'll look suspicious. Ever hear about not returning to the scene of a crime?"

"But Annie's cat is all alone. That man's gonna break the lock and sell Lester," she says.

"No one's gonna buy that cat. Besides, Lester'd just run away. And we've got two whole days. Right now we have to get back to Martha's. We've already been gone too long."

Martha's got breaded chicken in the oven, and mashed potatoes and peas all ready on the stove. She wants Sissy to set the table. Martha's singing along with an old Beatles song on the radio. "She's got a chicken to hide, but she don't care." Of course she's got the words wrong.

"Hungry?" she asks me.

"Yeah, smells good."

I'm worried she's going to ask a bunch of questions about what took us so long. But Martha gets so busy with Chance and dinner that I don't need to explain anything.

Martha piles more mashed potatoes on my plate and hands me the butter.

"I like to see a growing boy eat," she says.

I aim to please in that department. My belly feels a lot better since I've been staying with Martha. Everyone else is done with dinner so I finish off the rest of the potatoes and peas. Sissy wants to help with the dishes, but first Martha has to convince her to take off her sweater so it won't get wet. After the dishes Sissy tosses breadcrumbs to the pigeons out the living room window while Martha gives Chance his medicine. He makes a pucker face. It must taste weird.

"Uh-oh," Sissy says. She closes the window and runs to her room just as the doorbell rings.

"Can you get that, Soli?" Martha asks.

It's Sheila-not-Shelly, that awful new social worker. And she looks even grumpier than last time. I say hello but I don't offer to take her shoulder bag. It's so heavy she's standing there all lopsided. She's got her arms full of files too.

"Martha," I say. "We got a visitor."

artha is all fake friendly to Sheila-not-Shelly. Good thing Sissy and I got back in time.

"Nice of you to drop in again so soon," Martha says. She leads her into the living room and sits down with Chance on her lap.

"We just finished an early supper. Would you like some chicken?" Martha offers.

"No," says Sheila.

This lady never learned to say no thank you.

"This is an unannounced visit," rude Sheila says. She sneezes and unloads her pile of stuff onto Martha's coffee table.

"God bless you. Let me get you a tissue," Martha says.

Sheila wipes her eyes and sneezes again. "Do you have cats or any other pets on the premises?"

She looks around all suspicious, like Martha has a secret life as an animal trainer and we've got seven cages full of tigers in the back. Sissy stays in her room but she keeps poking her head out her door.

"No," Martha says. "No cats, no pets."

I notice Sissy's sweater on the back of the couch next to Sheila. Sissy was wearing it when she was holding that gigantic furry Lester on her lap. Then I see something else. The fat brown file on Martha's coffee table. Second one down in the stack. The fat brown file with my name on it.

I need to get that file. There's got to be information in there I don't know. Things I don't remember, from when I was Sissy's age. Or even younger. Like what happened to my parents and why I got stuck in foster care.

Sheila turns to Martha, opens a folder, and says, "I found some discrepancies and violations in your file. I don't know how Karen missed them. Your CPR and first aid certificates have—have . . ." She tries to stop herself from sneezing, but can't. She grabs a tissue. "Your certificates have expired."

Sheila writes something down, then she tries to stifle another sneeze.

"And what's that medication on the table?" She points her bony finger. "All medications must be inaccessible to children."

"Soli, could you please put the baby's medicine in the fridge?" Martha asks.

"All medications, *including* those requiring refrigeration must be under lock and—and—key. . . ." Sheila clicks her pen. "You need— need to . . ."

She has a herself a little sneezing fit and Martha keeps saying, "Bless you."

Then Sheila starts in again. "You need to install a lock on your refrigerator."

I put Chance's medicine in the fridge. Then I stand between the kitchen and the living room. I can't help staring at that big file with my name on it. I take a step forward and try to pick up Sissy's sweater without anyone noticing.

"Where are you going?" Sheila asks.

"I got homework for my summer job workshop tomorrow," I say, "and I promised Sissy I'd help with her dollhouse."

"Look, this is an official site inspection and I'll need to interview both of you for my report. Tell the other foster child to come out in five minutes."

Interview? Sounds more like an interrogation. I head down the hallway. But I'm still listening. That social worker keeps rattling off rules and wiping her eyes and nose with a tissue.

"And item seventeen, 'Children are to be transported by appropriately licensed drivers only.' I'll need a copy of your driver's license and current proof of insurance."

"Karen always told me, 'It's the big picture that counts,'" Martha says. "She looked at what was best for the children. Not all the little details."

"Those details are the law—laws enacted to protect children from harm," Sheila-not-Shelly says.

I go into Sissy's room and toss her the sweater.

"You have to come out," I whisper.

"Why?" She hugs her sweater, then eases her arms into it.

"Because we need to get rid of that social worker and get my file."

"What file?"

"The brown one. The second one down in her big pile of stuff. It's on the coffee table. Button up your sweater and grab that brown file, okay? Hide it under your sweater."

"No," says Sissy. "That's stealing. You do it."

"I can't. She'll suspect me, but not you. Besides, we're just borrowing it to take a look. It's my file—it's even got my name on it. If you don't help, that social worker will find a bunch of stuff wrong with how Martha's taking care of us."

Sissy stares at me.

"You like living here, don't you?" I say.

Sissy nods.

"Well, Sheila's like the big bad wolf's helper. She's gonna blow Martha's house down if we don't stop her. Are you gonna help or not?"

Sissy buttons her sweater, then tugs each sleeve down as far as it'll go.

"Okay, go sit right near Sheila. I'll distract her, then you knock over her stack of stuff. Grab my brown file, okay? Keep your back to her, and hide the file under your sweater."

Sissy twists her braid and nods again.

"The brown one, okay? I'll meet you later in Chance's room."

Sissy gathers her scissors and paper people. I go back to the living room where Sheila's finally stopped sneezing. But now she's harping on Martha about having enough food.

"And I can't allow one of your foster charges to lean out an open window to feed pigeons. Hundreds of children are injured every year in foster care. I won't let it happen on my watch."

Martha's jaw is tight. She's not talking.

"We live on the first floor," I say. "Sissy's not gonna fall out the window."

Chance hears my voice and waves his arms.

Sheila-not-Shelly glares at me and rearranges her files. Sissy comes in, dragging her whole cardboard dollhouse full of paper people. The minute Sissy sits on the floor that social worker starts sneezing like crazy again. Sissy's sweater must be covered in Lester's cat hair. Good thing it doesn't show.

Sissy reaches into her sweater pocket, pulls out her glue stick, and glues her fortune-cookie fortune to the box near one of the windows. Then she grabs her crayons and gets to work. She keeps her head down and draws a big tree and birds on the outside walls. Every time that social worker sneezes, Sissy's hand jerks and she stops drawing.

Sheila finally quits griping about Martha's violations because it's hard for her to talk and sneeze at the same time.

"Are you sure—there are no cats—on the premises?"

"Positive," says Martha. "Can I get you something?"

"A glass of water." Rude Sheila acts like Martha's her servant. She needs to learn some manners, and I'm going to teach her.

"I'll get it," I say.

Sissy looks up from her dollhouse, then ducks her head even lower, coloring more branches on her tree.

I get the biggest plastic cup we have—one of those thirty-two ouncers we got free at the gas station. I take my time, thinking through my plan as I fill the cup with water. I turn off the faucet and watch as Sheila fumbles in her purse for a bottle of pills.

Just as she spills a couple of pills into her hand, I take a little spill myself.

"Whoa," I say, as I stumble forward. Bull's-eye. She's soaked.

Sheila leaps up.

Sissy jumps up too. She knocks the stack of files onto the floor, grabs the brown one, and tucks it under her sweater. She's a pro.

Sissy runs down the hall yelling, "I'll get you a towel."

"Sorry," I say.

Sheila is shocked, Martha is shocked, and I'm half-shocked it actually worked. Nobody notices Sissy made off with my file.

I offer to get more water, but Sheila shouts, "No!" She's still not big on thank-yous. Martha stands up to help with Chance on her hip, and Sheila nearly pushes her aside. Sissy's back, handing a towel to the social worker, who looks like she's about to explode. Her voice comes out in stops and starts. "This—facility is—where is my pen?"

Her scary voice makes Chance cry.

"It's my fault," I say. "I must have tripped on something."

"Another violation I'll document—item twenty-seven, 'hazards in the home.'"

Martha tries to calm Chance. Sissy crawls on the floor pretending to look for Sheila's pen and messes up the files even more.

"Here it is," Sissy says, holding the pen in the air.

"Get away." Sheila grabs the pen from Sissy.

"Careful now," Martha says.

Too late. Sheila trips and lands on the couch, but not before one of her spiked heels comes down on Sissy's dollhouse, gashing a hole in the wall.

"You tore it," Sissy says.

"I—I'm . . . it's just a cardboard box," Sheila says. "The child should have appropriate toys. She shouldn't be playing with . . . trash."

Sissy goes silent. She puts her crayons, scissors, and paper people into the torn house and pulls it down the hall. Chance is ready to cry again. He scrunches up his face every time the social worker talks.

"Want me to take him to his room?" I ask Martha. "He doesn't like all this commotion."

"Thanks," Martha says. "Cha—I mean, Thaddeus is ready for his bottle. I'll get it."

I turn to Sheila. "I'm sorry," I say.

That's the truth. I'm sorry she's so clueless and rude. And I'm sorry she hasn't left yet.

She blots herself with Sissy's towel, but she's still soaked.

"Can I get you another towel?" I ask.

She ignores me.

Sissy is waiting for me in Chance's room.

I close the door and whisper, "Where's my file?"

"In a plastic bag. At the bottom of the diaper bucket. And I took that other paper too—the one she wrote down all Martha's bad grades on."

Sissy's smart. I put Chance in his crib and turn on his music box. He waves his little fingers at the mobile above his head.

I'm dying to read my file. But Sheila-not-Shelly's still here, and that all-wet social worker might notice it's missing. I can't risk getting caught. So I have to leave my file where it is.

For now.

CHAPTER 16

I f Martha knows we've been up to something, she's not saying anything. She finally gets the social worker out the door, then she starts
to give Chance a bath in the kitchen sink. Sissy drags a chair next to
Martha, kneels on it, and tries pushing up her sleeves.

"You've got your sweater on again?" Martha says.

Sissy darts her big eyes at me, then looks up at Martha all
innocent.

"Let's take if off for now," Martha tells her, "so you can help me
with Chance."

Sissy eases out of her sweater, hangs it over the chair, and sinks
those scarred arms of hers into the baby's bubbly bath water. She lath-
ers the soap and rubs Chance's arms.

"So what's the deal with that social worker?" I ask.

"She was sneezing so much she couldn't think straight," Martha
says. "Her list of out-of-compliance violations got lost in your little
water accident. Her papers got so mixed up she had to start from
scratch. She was soaking wet and she couldn't even remember what
she'd written the first time."

"Is that good or bad?" Sissy asks.

"Both," Martha says. "She'll be back, madder than ever, once
she reorganizes herself. In the meantime, I only got cited for two
things."

I want to go read my file. But I need to know what's happening
with the social worker. Like if she noticed anything missing.

"What'd she cite you for?"

"'Quality and quantity of food served.' She said I had 'an inade-quate supply.' She actually snooped in my cupboards and refrigera-tor. No canned corn or peaches like I usually have, no vegetables or fresh fruit. Just a bag of raisins, past their use-by date. She caught me at a bad time, that's all. It's the end of the month. She didn't need to look in my cupboards. Anyone with eyes can see my kids are well fed. Karen never snooped in my cupboards."

Chance splashes his hands in the water, then looks surprised when his face gets wet.

"What else did she cite you for?"

"Don't worry. Nothing they can shut me down for."

"Shut you down?" I ask. "They can't shut you down."

Sissy's hands go still in the water.

I've been stuck at foster homes a thousand times worse than Martha's. Somebody should have shut *those* places down.

"You ever been shut down before?" I ask.

Martha wraps Chance in a towel, kisses him on the forehead, and hugs him close.

She takes her time. She's stalling.

"Martha?" I ask.

"Just once," she says. "Don't worry. I'll give Karen a call."

Sissy looks worried enough for all of us. She's doing her super-silent thing like she's heading into her scary bad zone.

"So what else did Sheila-not-Shelly ding you on?"

"'Inappropriate toys and equipment,'" Martha says. "She never even looked in the toy box, so that's ridiculous. I can file an appeal on that one—easy. I got a ton of toys. And they're all appropriate."

Martha limps down the hall with Chance, toward his room, the diaper bucket, and my file.

71

"Sheila didn't like my dollhouse," Sissy says to me. "She broke it—she said it was trash."

"She doesn't know what she's talking about. That lady's mean. Come on, Sissy, let's go fix your house."

I grab Martha's duct tape and we head to Sissy's room. I have to keep busy or I'll go crazy waiting.

After we patch Sissy's house back together, I'm hoping I can get my file from Chance's diaper bucket, but I peek out of Sissy's room and Martha's still in there rocking and singing him to sleep. I should have grabbed it when they were giving him a bath.

"Soli, read me a story."

"Which one do you want?"

"*The Three Little Pigs*," she says.

"No way, not before bedtime. It'll give you nightmares again. That huffing and puffing wolf scares you, remember?"

"I'm bigger now," Sissy says. "And the pigs get away, right?"

"Yeah, the wolf gets boiled in a pot at the end, so he doesn't bother those pigs any more. But Martha got rid of that wolf book."

"I know where she hid it," Sissy whispers. Then she's gone and back in a flash with the book in her hands.

"You sure?" I ask.

Sissy hands me the book. "Read it," she says.

She sits next to me on the floor, bites her lower lip, and twists her braid through most of the story. I try not to make the wolf's voice too scary, especially in those huffing and puffing parts. But the pictures are scary all by themselves, with that drooling wolf and his sharp teeth. Not to mention when he gets boiled alive at the end. Larry would say, "That's a big X for you, Mr. Wolf. You shouldn't have gone down that chimney. You weren't thinking things through."

Sissy, she wants to study that last page for a while. Then she slams the book shut and runs to hide it back wherever Martha keeps it. I'm hoping Martha is out of Chance's room and Sissy will go to bed now so I can get my file. But Sissy's not tired. She wants to play with her paper doll people.

"Okay," I say. "But you got to stay in your room."

"I will," she says, but right as I'm closing her door Sissy calls me.

"Soli?"

I shouldn't have read her that big bad wolf story.

"What?"

"Will you check on me?"

"Yeah," I say. "In a little while." I head back out the door.

"Soli?"

"Now what?"

"Good night, Soli."

"Good night."

I look in Chance's room.

Martha is half asleep in the rocking chair with Chance snoozing on her chest. She's got her arms around him and even though he's asleep already, she's still rocking real slow.

"Hey, Martha," I say. "You should get to bed."

"Yeah," she says. "I don't know why I'm so tired."

She hands me the baby and I carry him to his crib. Chance opens his eyes and looks at me for just a second before he drifts back to sleep. He knows who I am.

Martha will guess something's up if I stay behind in Chance's room. Especially after our little interaction with that social worker. Martha's tired but she's not stupid. So I have to wait to get my file. And now she goes out to the living room, props up her bum leg on a bunch of pillows, and turns on the TV.

"Martha, you look beat. You should get some sleep."

"I'm gonna watch a little news first."

Chance's room is the first door off the living room. How am I going to nab my file without Martha noticing?

I sit on the arm of the couch. She's shaking her head at the TV, saying, "Soldiers all so young, some look too young to even shave. What are they doing over there? Fighting for what?"

Martha's talking to herself more than to me, so I just listen.

"Now young women over there. Who's going to take care of their kids?" Martha looks at me.

"I don't know, Martha."

"Reminds me of my Carl . . ." Martha's voice gets quiet.

"Who's Carl?"

Martha doesn't say, so I just wait. She turns off the TV and sighs.

"Carl was my husband. He went to Vietnam. He went off to Vietnam and never came back to me."

"He got killed in the war?"

Martha shakes her head. "We were going to start a family. He wanted a bundle of kids. I waited for him all that time—more than three years. That's a long time to worry and wait."

"What happened?"

Martha starts rubbing her knee and she's quiet. I wonder if I should say something or just leave her be. Then she looks up at me again. "He finally made it back."

"Yeah?"

Martha looks older all of a sudden.

"Yes, but after all the bad things he saw—it tortured his mind. After all my worrying and waiting for him—and waiting to start a family—after all he saw while he was overseas, Carl came back alive. Then he took his own life right here in San Francisco."

I don't know what to say. I reach for the box of tissues and hand it to Martha.

"So you never got married again?"

"No," Martha says. "But I've had more than a bundle of kids. I bet my Carl would have liked that. Don't you think?"

"Yeah," I say.

Martha pushes herself up from the couch and checks on Sissy, but she doesn't go to bed yet. Instead she puts away dishes in the kitchen where she's still got a view of the hallway and Chance's door. I think about my file and Martha's story about Carl.

Did my father go away to some war and never come back? Did my father want a bundle of kids? Did he want me?

CHAPTER 17

I stand a minute in the hallway hoping Martha's too distracted to notice me.

"Soli, you feeling okay?" She's staring right at me.

"Yeah, I'm okay. I was just thinking about my summer job workshop tomorrow. I better look over my homework."

"Good idea," she says, leaning over to rub her knee. "What time are you supposed to be there?"

"Ten."

"Maybe we could go to the farmers' market early before your workshop? Get some fresh produce to keep that social worker off my back?"

"Okay," I say. "If we're getting up early, we'd better get to bed then, right?"

"Right," Martha says. But she doesn't.

I head to my room and read the workshop sheet again. But I can't concentrate. The top of the first page says there are no right or wrong answers because these are "thinking exercises." Thinking exercises?

I'm thinking they better not collect my homework, because it's mostly blank.

It says to write down things I like and don't like. I already wrote down "cars" in the "I like . . ." section, even though there was room for a lot more than that. I add "taking things apart" and "building stuff."

I've got all kinds of things for the "don't like" section—I don't like stupid social workers writing down bad stuff about me for years and having no idea what they wrote. I don't like rude people like

Sheila-not-Shelly and that jerk at juvie clicking their pens over and over. I don't like not knowing if I ever had a mother or father, and if I did, why they never visited me. And if I had any parents, I bet I wouldn't have liked them either. They obviously didn't like or want me.

I don't like filling out forms. And how you always have to fill out forms to get stuff you need. I looked at the DMV website—how am I supposed to have both my parents sign the form for a permit when I don't even know who my parents are? I don't like not knowing if I'm mixed or biracial or what. I don't like it when teachers make us "share our family stories," because I've got no story.

I don't like not knowing what got me into foster care, and I don't like asking about it either. I don't like being moved around from one place to another, or being blamed for stuff I had nothing to do with. I don't like living where they lock up the food, steal your clothes, and push you around.

I don't like group homes with messed-up kids going off the deep end because of their mental problems and addictions—and I don't like watching those messed-up kids' families coming on visiting days. I don't like that Wired and I had to act like we didn't care about no one coming to see us. And I don't like counselors like Curly looking all pitiful and sorry for us either.

I don't like a lot of stuff, but I'm not writing it down. Because what's that got to do with getting a job? I leave that whole section blank.

The next page says to list three people I see as heroes and why. People in my family. What family? Or people in the news, sports, or politics. Whatever. I'm skipping that section.

The next page says to ask family and friends what they like and dislike about their jobs. Right. Who am I supposed to ask? Then there's space to list possible jobs related to what we wrote in our "thinking exercises." That's the last section, and I already filled it in with a list of car jobs.

I look in on Sissy again like I promised. She's in her pajamas sitting on her bed with her taped-back-together cardboard house. Sissy's coloring so fierce that the walls bend under the pressure of her crayons. She's drawing messy little red, orange, and black rectangles. Lots of them. And she squeezes those crayons so hard she already broke a few.

"What are you drawing?" I ask.

"Bricks," Sissy says. "I'm making my house out of bricks."

"Smart."

I watch her for a minute, then turn to leave.

"Good night, Soli."

"Good night."

Martha's finally asleep on the couch. I put a blanket over her 'cause she looks cold. I turn off the light, go straight to Chance's room and shut the door. He's sleeping soundly.

I get the plastic bag with my file and the list of Sheila-not-Shelly's complaints out of the smelly diaper bucket. I hide the papers under my shirt and head to my room.

Finally.

CHAPTER 18

My mind is racing.

I skim over the most recent reports from doctors, school counselors, social workers, group homes, and that idiot pen-clicking probation officer at juvie.

Then I find the old stuff. A birth certificate from the City of San Francisco, but it has lots of blanks—just like my workshop homework. Baby John Doe. It's got my birth date on it. Mother and father: unknown. Race: mixed/unknown. Weight: five pounds, three ounces. At least something is filled in.

Lots of doctor's reports—healthy, healthy, always healthy.

Then some official court documents and a news clipping.

They find me on a Greyhound bus. I'm just a couple of days old. No one knows exactly. "Abandoned," the newspaper says. My birth mother left me there. No one knows who she is.

A morning cleaning crew discovers me in the back of that Greyhound bus—at the downtown San Francisco bus station after all the passengers left. No one saw a pregnant woman. Or a baby.

But I'm that baby. Baby John Doe.

They don't know if my mother got on the bus somewhere between New York and San Francisco or if she snuck on board the parked bus and left me there. I'm wrapped in a man's jacket in a car-parts box on the floor in the last row of seats. No note. No clothes. No blanket. Nothing. Just me and that jacket.

The passengers left. The man with the jacket left. My mother left me too. I was just a baby and they all left me.

I'm crying when they find me.

And I'm hungry.

The article says, "Police speculate the infant might have been alone, crying, and hungry all night long."

An investigator is assigned to the case but there are no leads and no witnesses.

Someone named Mrs. Luz de la Paz, a San Francisco widow, calls the news, calls the police, calls Child Protective Services. She claims to be my "paternal grandparent," the paper says. Other people call. They all want me. Or at least they did then.

I keep reading.

Mrs. Luz de la Paz tries again and again to gain custody—of me. The court grants Mrs. Luz de la Paz temporary custody. Is she the lady with the yellow towels? Maybe my first memory—sitting in a basket of warm towels from the dryer.

I stay with my grandmother "until the child's birth mother can be located," the documents say.

But a year later—birth mother still unknown.

Father's whereabouts unknown.

Mrs. Luz de la Paz and her neighbors were questioned. The neighbors say she had three, maybe four sons, and some nephews living there, too—whereabouts all unknown. There are more doctors' and social workers' reports dated a couple of years later.

I find another birth certificate with the same birth date, but this one has my name filled in—Solomon de la Paz. Middle name left blank. Mother's and father's names still blank.

Then Mrs. Luz de la Paz dies.

The Department of Social Services still can't find my birth mother or father. I become a ward of the State of California.

I'm three years old.

A psychologist's report says it is believed that I speak Spanish, but I refuse to talk. It says I am grieving the loss of my grandmother. I don't remember any Spanish-speaking grandmother. But maybe that's why Spanish has always been easy for me—without even studying.

After that psychologist's report, it's one foster home after another. All those people who wanted me when I was a baby must have disappeared because after Mrs. Luz de la Paz dies, no one wants me.

I don't know what I was expecting to find in my file. I look at the papers again and again—and now I have more questions.

Why'd my mother leave me on that bus? If she didn't care about me, then why'd she wrap me up? Was my mother wearing a man's jacket to hide being pregnant? Did she even tell my father? Would he have come for me if he knew?

Were they both coming to San Francisco to live with my grandmother? Did they change their minds or what? Didn't any of the passengers hear me cry? Or was I like Chance when he first got to Martha's—with his voice so weak, so little air in his lungs, that you could barely hear him?

And was that Luz lady really my grandmother? She must have wanted me, otherwise she wouldn't have gone to court to petition for custody. And she kept me for three years. Who was with her when she died? And who was taking care of me?

I don't remember. I don't like not knowing.

But there's nothing I can do about it.

CHAPTER 19

There are more papers, forms, and reports in my file—like the recent situations. But most of it is all wrong.

I look at the reports by Larry, Curly, and Moe, the rotating counselors at my last group home—the Three Stooges House, we called it—where I lived with Wired and those other guys.

Those counselors never knew what we called them behind their backs, even though Curly was big on analyzing people's nicknames. Larry's name really was Larry. He was in charge. He cooked the best too—especially his cornbread and stew.

"Misfit boys gotta eat," he always said.

That's the truth, but nobody bothered to write down my favorite meals in my file. Instead, there's a psychological report by that lady counselor we called Curly. That report makes no sense, just like Curly.

Curly had frizzy hair, long skirts, and jewelry clinking on her wrists, and she'd always look at you deep—too deep, right in your eyes—and ask, "How does that make you feel?" Curly was all right, but not so smart at first. I thought you had to be smart to go to college. She left her purse in the closet that first day and then acted all hurt when most of her money was gone. Didn't even appreciate that she still had bus money to get home. Larry didn't appreciate it either. Since nobody fessed up to taking her money, he took away the TV. I felt bad later, when I got to know her, but not at first.

Curly didn't have a clue. She tried to lead us in group discussions. Tried to make us to talk about what we'd done to land us in a group home—but of course we all just wanted to forget about that. Curly said we'd feel better if we shared our feelings, plans, and goals. She was big on sharing—too bad no one was ever in the mood to talk. Sometimes she had topics jotted down in her notebook—like analyzing nicknames. She asked why Wired was called Wired, as if you couldn't tell just by talking to the dude for five minutes. She wanted to know why everyone called me Shifty, and so on with all the other guys. But she never figured out she was Curly, even after we got our TV privileges back and we were falling on the floor laughing at the *Three Stooges* video.

Curly was disappointed I wasn't pouring my heart out to her. I wasn't the only one not talking. When the house was full, there were seven of us not talking. She tried to get us to write in journals. That didn't work, so she pulled out board games and cards. But someone always cheated and then the furniture would be falling, and she'd have to call Moe in to break it up.

Moe was good at that. Big scary guy—he'd probably been in prison, because he was always saying, "You want to be tough? Want to go to jail? Keep it up, you'll see what it's like."

Moe didn't have many skills besides shouting "Break it up," and whomping on anybody who wasn't listening. I don't remember his real name either, but I remember his face, the scar above his eyebrow, and the knife through a bleeding heart tattoo on his arm. If I saw a guy like Moe walking down the street, I'd find a reason to cross to the other side.

One afternoon Curly showed up with a stack of books. None of us were big on reading, so she read aloud from an old book of Native American tales. Some were about a shape-shifter trickster guy that could change from a human to a coyote, then to a woodpecker, and a wasp, and sometimes a raven or a bear—always tricking the other animals. The shape-shifter would get the better of them, but it ended up for the animals' own good. After I left the group home and had been at Martha's awhile, I figured out Curly probably read those shape-shifter stories for me.

Larry's the one that got Wired the job at Starbucks. I went to Larry's office and told him I wanted to make some cash too.

He thumbed through my file and said, "Might be a mistake for you and Wired to work at the same place. Besides, it seems you need to be around cars, not coffee."

Whatever.

"If you sign this contract not to mess up for a month," he said, "I'll find a car connection for you."

Yeah, right. I didn't trust him.

"Something you can build on," Larry said. "And get some job skills."

"Like what?"

"Lots of options with cars," Larry said. "Mechanic's shop, auto body, detailing, maybe something in a new car dealership. Lots of possibilities—if you stay on track."

Then Larry went back to the condition of me not messing up, and told his story about the pad of paper and the big X.

"Imagine your life as a small pad of paper," Larry said. "Days go by—and you and your pad of paper are just fine. But each time you do something stupid without thinking, you have to tear a page off the pad. And somewhere on one of those upcoming pages there is a big thick X. Like a big fat mistake, and then there's no going back."

"I know, Larry, we never know when the X page is coming up."

"Right. That big X might be at the top of the pad, or somewhere in the middle, or near the bottom. You never know. So you got to think smart and avoid making mistakes."

Larry liked that story, and he didn't see any harm in repeating it over and over.

One time Wired interrupted him in the middle of his story. "Yeah, Larry. We heard this before, but what *is* the big X?"

"You'll know when you see it," Larry said.

It took me two months before I stopped messing up enough for Larry to find me a job. Of course there's a report about that in my file, and a copy of my not-messing-up contract. But they got it all wrong. I wasn't out of control. I knew exactly what I was doing. I had to jump on Moe's back to keep him from whomping on Wired. That wasn't my fault, but it set me back another month. And the job Larry got me? Something to build on? Vacuuming cars at the Daly City car wash and wiping them dry.

I stay up half the night reading the stuff in my file, including some recent forms filled out by Karen and Sheila-not-Shelly. The idiot Juvenile Hall officer wrote reports about those mix-ups at the two foster homes where I stayed before the Three Stooges House. But he got it all wrong. Yeah, there was a gun in Pat and Louise's glove box. And yeah, there was a knife at Janice's place. But neither of those situations was my fault.

"You got a bad track record with weapons," that juvie officer kept saying. "I'm right, am I not?"

I had nothing to do with any weapons.

I get agitated just thinking about that jerk at Juvenile Hall, so I leave my room and walk around Martha's house. Martha must have dragged herself off to bed. And she was right about needing to go to the farmers' market. We better go to the grocery store too. There's nothing left in the refrigerator except some cheese, bread, a half carton of milk, and cold chicken. I eat those last three pieces of chicken, then head back to my room.

I look in on Sissy. She's asleep, curled up at the bottom of her bed. There's no room for her because she's got her cardboard house in there. Her paper people are all lined up on her pillow like they are marching off to some weird family reunion. I ease a crayon out of her hand and move her house to her desk. I don't want her to squash it.

I scoop up her paper dolls. I look at those cardboard people for a second, and then I place them in one of Sissy's dollhouse rooms. She can move them how she wants in the morning. I scoot Sissy up so her head's on the pillow. She pulls the blanket around herself, eyes still closed, and goes right on sleeping.

I go in Chance's room. It's cool and dark except for the glow of his night-light, but he looks warm and comfortable. I sit in Martha's chair for a minute and watch him snooze. I wonder what he's remembering right now in his baby head. Chance sighs in his sleep.

"I hear you, buddy," I say. "At least no one left you on a Greyhound bus."

CHAPTER 20

I must have fallen asleep in the middle of the night rereading all those papers. When I wake up in the morning one of the pages is half stuck to my face, and the rest are spread around my room. I put everything back in the folder and hide it in my closet under my *Car & Truck* magazines.

When I get to the kitchen Martha is singing along with the radio again. "Ain't no woman like a one-eyed goat." After the first stanza it starts to sound right.

Sissy plays with her dollhouse people on the kitchen floor and Martha is giving the baby a little massage at the table. She's talking to him, telling him he's doing great.

"That's it, Chance. Stretch those arms up. Feels good, huh?"

Those exercises are supposed to make him less shaky. I'm eating my cold cereal when Martha looks up and sees me staring at them.

"Don't ever do drugs, Solomon."

I don't want to hear about drugs and I don't want her calling me Solomon either. I drop my bowl in the sink. I know plenty about how drugs mess you up. Half the guys at the Three Stooges House were messed up from drugs.

And way before that, J.J., that idiot boyfriend of Janice's, ruined my foster situation with her. I was there from ten to thirteen years old, going to school, making friends, and even getting good grades. Everything steady. But then J.J. started using and acting crazy for no reason. Then Janice was doing drugs right along with him. They were fighting all the time, and then one day—one day Janice hauled off and stabbed him.

I think Janice's own girl, Lucy, was taken away by social services after that. I remember Lucy and me standing at their front door. Lucy was little, maybe six or seven—about the same age Sissy is now—and she was holding my hand, saying, "What are we gonna do?"

I didn't know. After I called 911 and said we needed an ambulance, I didn't know what else to do. J.J. was all cut and bloody, sitting on the curb, staring into the sky. Janice was trying to hide the knife some-where. And when the ambulance and the police came, I lied.

I didn't want to get Janice in trouble so I said I didn't see what happened.

Maybe they hauled Janice and J.J. both off to jail—after they stitched him up. I don't know. I never saw Janice or her little girl, Lucy, again. I never got to finish the school year with my friends. Instead I got carted off to a different school in another town, then spent my thirteenth birthday with people I didn't even know.

So Martha doesn't need to lecture me about drugs. I don't do drugs—never have, never will. And she better not call me Solomon anymore. I told her when I first got to her place to call me Shifty like the guys at the group home, but Martha refused. So Martha and Sissy call me Soli—I thought she got that. So why'd she call me Solomon? When I was little, everyone called me Sol or Soli. Some teachers try to call me Solomon when they first meet me, but I make sure they switch to Soli pretty quick.

Not that jerk at juvie. He called me Solomon right off and never let up, opening and closing my file, clicking his stupid pen, and leaning back in his chair. And when I told him I didn't like it, he switched to Solo-Man, and kept harassing me about being alone in the world.

"Solo-Man, it says here you were abandoned by your mom—that's too bad. Then you were so difficult nobody else wanted you. What do you have to say about that?"

I didn't say anything. I tried to ignore him by looking out his window. My room at Juvenile Hall didn't have any windows. And all the doors were locked like some kind of jail.

"You got to work with me here, Solo-Man. Because any fool can see—you got nobody. You are nobody. That's rough, Solo-Man. No family, and you're messing up with everyone who ever tried to help you."

"It says here," that idiot probation officer continued, "it says here you were involved in a stabbing situation, but you didn't see what happened. How can that be, Solo-Man?"

I shook my head. I wasn't telling him anything. Especially not how I saw Janice stab J.J. with his own stupid knife. I didn't tell her to stab him, even though he deserved it. And I didn't choose to get sent all over the place. But I didn't explain any of that to that jerk at juvie. I just ignored him.

"Solo-Man, you listening? What's the matter with you? You got a communication problem? You can't talk like other people? Or you just got a bad attitude, Solo-Man?"

Solo-Man this, Solo-Man that. When I wouldn't answer, he started clicking his pen.

"And why'd you steal your last foster mom's truck and gun? Who were you planning to rob? Not even fourteen years old, and stealing a vehicle. I don't have to point it out to you, do I? That's just plain stupid, Solo-Man. How far did you think you'd get?"

I didn't want to say anything with him calling me Solo-Man, but I couldn't stop myself. He was pissing me off.

"I told you that was all a mix-up. Pat and Louise let me move the truck down the driveway every week to wash it. One day I just drove a little farther. I didn't know Pat owned a gun, or that she'd locked it in the truck."

"Once again, Solo-Man, you're full of excuses."

"I told you, it was locked in the glove box and I never tried to open it. I didn't even know it was there."

He leaned back in his chair, clicked his pen, and opened my file again. "Says here you stole their truck and gun. What's wrong with you?"

I had to listen to him, his Solo-Man, and his stupid clicking pen for three months before they replaced him. After that I hated anyone calling me Solomon. So when the guys at the Three Stooges House started calling me Shifty because of my talent for getting out of things and switching chores, that was fine with me.

Of course Martha doesn't know about that jerk at juvie. She doesn't know Sissy took my file last night, or that it's filled with false reports about me. Maybe that stuff about Baby John Doe isn't true either.

"Soli, what's bothering you?" Martha asks.

"Nothing."

"Then why are you crunching up the box so tight when there's still cereal in it?"

I look down at my hands. I've rolled the top of the box down until it can't go any farther.

Martha comes over, still holding Chance, and takes the cereal box from me.

"I can tell you're thinking about something important," Martha says. She touches my shoulder and sets the squished box on the counter.

"Yeah, well—just call me Sol or Soli, okay?"

"Did I say Solomon again? I'm sorry. I didn't mean to harp on you about drugs either. I know you're clean. You've got nothing to do with Chance's problems. I trust you to make good decisions."

She's trusting me to make good decisions.

Yeah, right.

CHAPTER 21

A little later Martha pulls her ancient vacuum out of the closet.

"Soli, can you go to the farmers' market for me before your workshop? Or walk to the produce store on Mission? I'd go too, but I need to clean up the house in case Sheila comes snooping around. We're low on fruit."

Low? More like completely out.

"Okay," I say.

Sissy looks up from her cardboard people.

"Can I walk with Soli to the store?" Sissy asks.

"Okay, but come back quick so Soli can get to his workshop at eleven."

My job class starts at ten but I don't tell Martha. Maybe I'll skip it entirely.

"And could you both bring me your sheets and towels, please? I'm starting a load of laundry."

Sissy hops up and starts dragging her dollhouse away. "Martha, should I hide this in my closet and put out some toys?"

"Yes, maybe so," Martha says. "But Sissy, you play with your dollhouse whenever you feel like it, you hear?"

Sissy nods.

Martha opens her wallet. It's nearly empty.

"Okay, we need apples, peaches, and some kind of vegetable," she says. "Just a few things to last us until I get my checks the first of July. Just get whatever's cheap. Thanks."

Martha is distracted, plugging in the vacuum one minute, sorting piles of laundry the next, so she doesn't see Sissy take the keys to the van.

I follow Sissy out the door.

"You're gonna get us in trouble," I say. But I like how Sissy's getting sneakier.

"Come on," Sissy says. "Lester's hungry, so don't spend all the money on fruit."

I unlock the van and Sissy climbs in.

"We might not have time for Lester this morning," I say.

"Start driving." Now Sissy's sneaky *and* bossy.

We get to the farmers' market and drive around the perimeter. Parking is bad as usual.

"Hurry up, Soli. Look, there's a spot."

"We can't park in front of a fire hydrant."

"Give me the money," Sissy says. "You park. I'll buy the fruit."

No way am I letting her out alone, especially after our Scary Mary Poppins incident. I circle around again looking for a parking space. I finally see a bunch of people parking in the Cheap Suits lot across from the farmers' market. The store is boarded up like it's been closed for years.

We park, then Sissy's out of the van, speed-walking toward the crowd. She stops in front of the Chinese stall to stare at the live chickens, crawling-around turtles, and every kind of stinky dead fish you can imagine.

"Let's get fish heads for Lester," Sissy says.

"We have to buy Martha's stuff first."

"How about those purple things?"

"Eggplants?" I say. "What if Martha doesn't know how to cook them?"

Sissy shrugs and walks on through the crowd. We choose some

apples and peaches. I give the guy money, and while he's making change I glance to the right for vegetables.

Last week I called the Three Stooges House to try to find Wired. He's not there anymore and they wouldn't tell me where he went. Now I see him—skinny Wired in his oversized tie-dyed shirt. It's him, way down by the flower lady.

"Sissy, get the change," I say and I start after him.

"Wired," I call.

He doesn't hear me. I run to catch up to him without knocking anyone over.

"Wired," I call again. He turns sideways but it's not him—the guy doesn't look like Wired at all now. Even the colors on his tie-dyed shirt are wrong.

I head back to Sissy.

"Give me the change," I tell her.

"No. I'm saving it for Lester's fish heads."

"Hand it over."

She gives me two dollars and keeps the rest.

"Sissy, I need more than two bucks for vegetables."

But she refuses. So I'm looking around for something cheap. I see onions and all kinds of greens, but nothing I've ever seen Martha cook. It's a regular United Nations. Not many people are speaking English, but I hear Spanish, Chinese, and some other languages I don't recognize, like Russian maybe. Little kids in strollers and people with their rolling carts crowd the sidewalk and it's getting harder and harder to walk around.

Potatoes. Finally something Martha cooks, and they're cheap too. I pay the guy and he hands me a bag full of different-colored potatoes. I turn around but a bunch of ladies are crowding in behind me.

"Sissy? Where'd you go?"

Some people turn. But no Sissy.

"Sissy?" I say louder.

Where is she?

"Sissy!" I shout.

"Soli," she says. She's waving at me, sitting with a bunch of little kids on the curb. They're all watching an old lady on some kind of go-cart music-making contraption. The old lady's short hair is sticking out of her farmer-style baseball hat. She's so old and wrinkled she could be homeless Annie's great-grandmother. Especially with that hat, checkered shirt, and her patched-up jeans.

The strangest thing of all—and what's got all the kids mesmerized—is the way she's bending a saw and drawing a bow across it to make music. A scratchy cassette deck plays background music like no one in this century listens to, but it's got a beat. She sets the saw down, and now she's tapping some jangly spoons on her knee.

A couple of kids get up from the curb to dance. That music lady, she's older than old, but when she smiles at those dancing kids—it rearranges all the wrinkles on her face so she doesn't look so ancient anymore. A crowd gathers around with more kids, and more dancing, and other little kids are swaying on their mamas' hips.

The music lady switches instruments again to a smaller saw and runs the bow across the flat side of that. She's strong the way she bends that saw. She's wearing faded-green garden gloves—to protect her hands from the saw blade, I guess. The small saw makes high notes that float in the air under the fog and just above all the languages and people smiling and dancing and stopping to watch. It's kind of eerie— the sounds that wrinkled old woman draws out of that saw.

I look to see if Sissy is going to dance. I've never seen her dance— she's usually carrying around too much leftover sadness on her skinny shoulders to dance—and she's not dancing now. Sissy's sitting tight on the curb next to a small Chinese kid with his shiny hair sticking straight up like a bristle brush. He's not dancing either.

Then the old lady starts tapping her foot on a pedal connected to a mechanical wooden cat with hinged legs—so the cat is dancing too. Dancing to the beat. The kids' eyes grow big in unison. The Chinese kid looks at his mama, points to the jiggling cat, and then holds his mama's hand. Sissy looks at the dancing cat. She looks at the kid and his mama. And as much as Sissy likes watching that jazzy cat with the clackety feet, she can't stop staring at the way the little boy and his mama are holding hands.

A bunch of people clap and put money in the old lady's toolbox. It reminds me of an offering in a church I went to with one of my old foster families. Of course Martha didn't give us much money. But Sissy pulls some coins out of her pocket and they go clinking into the rusty toolbox. The old lady nods and reaches for a guitar with a metal washboard behind the strings. Even though my bags are heavy, I want to hear how that sounds.

But I hear a commotion behind me. The potato seller is pointing to the Cheap Suits parking lot. "Hey," he shouts. "They're towing cars!"

"Come on, Sissy!" I pick her up and we take off running.

She's light and I can go faster through the crowd carrying her. The bags of potatoes, apples, and peaches are whomping against my leg. I run as fast as I can, considering all that I'm carrying.

But I'm not fast enough.

CHAPTER 22

Three tow trucks block the exit to the parking lot. A mean-looking guy is chuckling and pointing to rusted tow-away signs around the lot.

"Can't you read?" he says. "What part of *No Parking,* don't you get?"

People are shouting as one truck tows a silver minivan away. Two more tow trucks back in.

I set Sissy down and she slides her hand into mine. "What're we gonna do?" she says.

I look around.

"They don't have enough tow trucks for all these cars," I say. "Come on."

We slip past the crowd and into the lot. One truck driver has his back to us. He pulls a big cable with a monster-sized hook from the back of his ancient dented truck. Tow trucks aren't supposed to use hooks like that anymore. He'd better attach it to some other car. We sneak around the side of our van and I open up the driver's door, real quiet. Sissy climbs into her seat. I drop the bags next to her, slide in, and slouch down low. The trucks are blocking the only exit. I don't know how we'll get out.

Something makes a terrible noise under our rear axle. "What's that?" Sissy says. Our car jerks and it feels like we're being lifted off the ground.

"Put your seat belt on, Sissy, and don't unlock your door no matter what."

I lock my door too.

"Stay there. Face front." I crawl into the back of the van.

"Where are you going?" Sissy whispers. She cranes her neck to watch me.

A heavy door slams, and our van thumps back to the ground.

"What the hell?" someone shouts. Whoever he is, he's close. "Get out of the car, kid!" He pounds on Sissy's door. "We're towing this one!"

"Don't move, Sissy," I say. I don't know if she can hear me or not.

Sissy's not saying a thing and I can't see what's going on up there. I peer out the back window. There's a slack cable between the van and his rusty tow truck. I can hear the truck's engine humming.

Sissy startles me by leaning on our horn. I pull the handle on the back door, jump out, and crawl under our van. The driver's heavy boots are outside Sissy's door. My heart's thumping louder than he's pounding on her door. I crawl commando style and lift the hook off our axle.

"Come on, kid. Get out!" he shouts at Sissy. "I ain't gonna hurt you."

Stay put, Sissy, I think. *Stay put.*

I set the chain down as quietly as I can. Bits of gravel scratch my hands and belly, making noise as I crawl back out, but Sissy is pounding on the horn so much, I guess he can't hear me. I bang my head on the bumper getting up. My heart is racing. I see through the van and out the windshield. Sissy's honking is attracting people, but the tow truck guy is so busy yelling and pounding on her door that he doesn't notice.

His truck door is wide open and I want to run over, grab his keys, and toss them in the bushes. Wired would, if he was here. That'd slow the driver down—prevent him from towing me or anyone else away. But I have to watch out for Sissy. I crawl into the back of Martha's van and the rear door creaks. Sissy's still honking like a maniac. I pull the door shut and lock it. He must have heard, because now he's running to the back, rattling the back-door handle.

Locked.

He grabs the side door and sticks his hairy face close to the window. Can he see me through the tinted glass?

Boom! He kicks the side door hard with those clomper boots of his. It nearly knocks me over.

Sissy screams, "You better stop that. My bodyguard-nanny knows jujitsu. She's gonna beat you up for kicking our car! She's gonna be here any minute—with her jujitsu friends!"

The dude goes back around to the driver's door. Sissy leans on the horn again. It's sounding weaker—more like a sick goose than a car horn.

I leap over the bag of peaches and baking soda into the driver's seat just as the guy is grabbing my door handle. I thump down on the lock again, just in case.

"Hey, punk—get the hell out of there! I'm towing this heap."

My hand is shaking as I turn the key in the ignition and press on the clutch.

Un-nun-nun-nun-nun. The van won't start.

"Go, Soli. Go!" Sissy says.

The guy is thumping on my door now. He's just inches away and he is pissed off.

Un-nun-nun-nun-nun.

"Stupid punk. You're not going anywhere. Your battery's dead, and you're chained to my rig."

What would Wired do? Probably get himself arrested somehow.

Un-nun-nun-nun-nun.

"Leave those kids alone," someone shouts from the crowd.

"What'dya gonna do about it?" He turns his ugly face away from me.

Splat! A tomato flies past him and oozes down my window. But the next tomato hits him. It's the Chinese mama and a grandma too, along with a whole bunch of Chinese tomato-throwing teens. The tow truck driver ducks, but two more tomatoes connect. He lumbers toward their car, practically growling.

"Back off—or I'm calling the cops," another man in the crowd shouts. He's got his cell phone out and he's punching in numbers.

The tow truck driver looks up and stares at all the people gathering.

The Chinese mama and grandma put that little spiky-haired kid in the backseat of their Toyota and pile in after him. The teens jump in quick, and the four doors slam shut. Then that Toyota veers across the sidewalk, bumps over a curb, and zips into the street.

"Hey," shouts the truck driver. He takes a few steps after them, wiping his shirt, but they're gone.

I'm still turning the key and giving it gas.

Un-nun-nun-nun-nun.

"Please-please-please." Sissy's got her eyes closed, and she's rocking her skinny body forward and back.

Un-nun-nun-nun-nun. Maybe I flooded it.

The tow truck driver turns around, even madder than before. He stomps toward us.

This is bad. When the police come, I'll be stuck between an angry tow truck driver and cops asking to see my license.

Un-nun-nun-nun-nun. My fingers can't squeeze any tighter around the key. My mouth is dry, and I got a bad feeling in my belly.

"Please-please-please," Sissy is whispering again.

I hear a trace of that old lady's saw music hanging in the air— and next thing I know, we lurch into reverse. *Boom!* We crash into the bumper of his tow truck behind us.

"What the hell?" He runs to his rig but I'm already shifting into first and following the Toyota's route over the curb.

It's bumpy but we are *out* of there. Fastest two-point turn I ever made.

I glance in the rearview mirror and the tow truck guy is lifting his cable with the big hook off the ground. He tilts his head like he has no idea how the dumb thing fell off. I hear people clapping but I can't look because I have to keep my eyes on the road.

I give it some gas, and we're catching up to that Toyota heading onto a freeway ramp. I have no idea where we're going. I glance at Sissy and she's waving to the little spiky-haired kid in front of us. He waves back until his hand-holding mama turns him back around in his booster seat.

"You got your seat belt on?" I ask.

"Yeah," says Sissy. "But you don't."

I buckle up and take a deep breath. I check the rearview mirror again.

"We have to drive around," I say. "Until the battery recharges."

Sissy nods.

"That was smart of you—pounding on the horn to draw attention away from me," I say.

She nods again.

"You were brave too," I say.

"Yeah," Sissy says with a big sigh. And now she's almost smiling.

I turn on the radio. Martha's oldies station is playing that "Hot Rod Lincoln" song with the police siren sound effects and crazy guitar solo. I wonder if the old saw lady—I mean, the lady with the saws—knows how to play this song.

I turn up the volume and the radio blares our getaway music.

CHAPTER 23

We don't have time to check on Lester. When we get back, Martha makes me take the Muni bus downtown to my workshop. By the time I get to the building on Van Ness Avenue and find the right room, I'm more than an hour late. The lady leading the workshop tells me to call her Joanne. I sit alone at a table in the back of the room full of magazines, scissors, and papers.

Joanne asks to see my homework, but of course it's mostly blank. She glances over my list of car jobs, passes out paper, and instructs everyone to "draw a road map of your life so far."

I look around the room, and everyone but me is starting to draw.

"On your road map, I want you to mark important events in your life," she says.

Sure, lady. Let's see, I can draw a Greyhound bus, a box with a baby in it and some lady running away. Then a whole row of run-down houses with nobody home. Then juvie with no windows. Yeah, right. I'm not drawing any of that.

"Nice, very nice," Joanne the Job Lady says, as if drawing a map is the key to the best-paid jobs in the world. She's walking around the room. "Take your time. There is no right or wrong way."

I should have sat closer to the door so I could get the heck out of here. I try to tune her out. Other people move around, go get magazines and scissors, and cut things out at their seats, all while she's jabbering away. I check the clock. I promised Sissy I'd buy Lester some food with the rest of our farmers' market money. I wonder if Job-Lady Joanne took roll already.

"Having trouble getting started?" she says. "I can help."

"No thanks," I say. I reach for a magazine and start flipping through pages, looking for a car to cut out. "Did you take roll?"

She nods. "I marked you here," she says. "But tomorrow, please be on time."

I cut out a silver mustang convertible with mag wheels and glue it on my paper. She wanders away, so I flip through the old newspapers. Martha used to cut out news articles when I first got to her place. She'd leave them on the kitchen table next to the milk and Corn Flakes so I couldn't avoid them. They were usually stories about a dumb kid who did something stupider than usual and ended up paying for it with jail time, or in some other tragic way.

"I bet he never expected that could happen when he woke up that day," Martha would say. "It's a crying shame."

Or she'd cut out a story about an unexpected genius do-gooder or some hero who rescues a whole family from drowning. Martha would say about those hero people, "I bet he's just an average person. Average every day of his life. And inside him, a hero is brewing all along, just waiting for the opportunity to do some good."

She used to make me read all those news articles, and then she'd want to know what I thought.

I never had much to say.

"Yep, that's a shame," I'd say. Or, "He's a hero, all right." Best to agree. I didn't want to get into a big discussion. When Martha left those articles for me to read, she reminded me of Curly—the annoying part of Curly.

But ever since Sissy and Chance arrived at Martha's, she's had less time for cutting stuff out. I don't think she even gets the newspaper anymore.

The weird thing is, I kind of miss her clippings.

So it feels good to space out reading the paper while Job-Lady Joanne talks on and on. I read one news article, then start another. I'm into the first paragraph and I don't want to read any more. Some sixteen-year-old kid—they won't name on account of him being a minor—stole a car. The police chased him all over the city. He swerved over the curb and nearly crashed into a building. Two police cars pulled up and blocked his escape. One cop got out to arrest him. But the kid wouldn't give up. Instead, the kid backed up, trying to get out of there. And when the cop's arm got pinned between two cars, the other cops started shooting. Now the kid is dead.

That could have been Wired. Wired stole cars before he came to the group home, and he talked about doing it again. He tried to get me to go with him, but I talked him out of it, especially after my own mix-up with Pat and Louise's truck and how that landed me in juvie. When Wired drank too many of those coffee drinks, he couldn't think straight. I convinced him we should wait—plan a real road trip instead, save some money, get our licenses, and buy a cheap car. Emancipate ourselves out of the system and head to Las Vegas, the Grand Canyon, or someplace we've never been.

Cops shouldn't shoot a kid like that.

Martha didn't cut this article out for me, but I'm hearing what she'd be saying, and I'm hearing it in her voice. *It's a crying shame.*

Joanne's still talking. "Okay, imagine your life five years from now. Where will you be living? Who will you be living with? Will you be in college or in the workforce? What kind of job will you have? Write that down on your road map."

Five years from now? I'll be twenty years old. I have no idea what I'll be doing.

"Good work, everybody," Joanne says. "Tomorrow we'll continue our discussion about informational interviews, making a good impression, and job shadowing. I'll see you all tomorrow morning." She looks right at me. "At ten."

I can't get out of there fast enough.

CHAPTER 24

Typical San Francisco summer weather—it's just past noon and the fog is already rolling back in, misty and cold. I buy cat food at a drug store on Van Ness. By the time I catch the bus, the wind is blowing like crazy. Papers are soaring up and down Mission Street, and ladies' dresses are flying every which way. At least that makes the view from the bus more interesting.

When I get back, Martha tells me Sissy's playing at Darlene's and could I get back on Muni to pick her up at two o'clock because Chance is snoozing.

Martha says, "I could use a little nap myself."

Martha looks worn out. She's rubbing her knee again. But the house looks better than it did this morning.

"Okay," I say.

"Thanks. And Soli, no more driving the van without me," Martha says.

"What if it's an emergency?" I say.

"I'm not anticipating any emergencies, but should one arise, we'll do whatever we have to do. Got it?" Martha says.

"Yeah."

Martha wipes down the kitchen counters. "By the way," she says, "I called Karen because that new social worker's got me worried."

Me too. I'd like to figure out a way to get rid of Sheila-not-Shelly.

"What'd Karen say?"

"I got her machine," Martha says. "So I left a message."

"Hey, Martha, how many times has Sheila been here snooping around?"

"Twice. You were here both times. And as far as I'm concerned, she's been here two times too many."

I pick up Martha's pen from her telephone table and click it while I think.

"So she never came by while me and Sissy were at school?" I ask.

"No . . . why?"

"Just wondering about some stuff," I say.

I've been thinking about Sheila a lot since I read my file. I never thought much about my social workers before, but now that we're stuck with Sheila-not-Shelly harping on us, I realize Karen never gave me or Martha any grief.

Martha sits down at the kitchen table. "What happened to these apples and peaches?" she asks. "They're all bruised."

She thinks we went shopping on Mission Street so I'm not explaining what happened at the farmers' market.

"I guess I could make my Aunt Ellen's cobbler," Martha says. "Maybe later. Right now I'm beat."

Martha opens the refrigerator, looks at the empty shelves, and sighs. "After you pick up Sissy, get some burgers for the two of you, and bring me one too, please." She gives me some money from the not-so-secret jug she hides in the cupboard.

"I should be getting some checks any day now," Martha says. "As long as the Fourth of July holiday doesn't hold up the mail."

Martha gives me enough for burgers but not enough for bus fare. The way I figure it is, if we don't feed that cat it'll croak, which would be an emergency as far as Sissy is concerned. It'd take too long on Muni to pick up Sissy, get to the storage place, feed the cat, and get back to Martha's.

Martha's so tired, she's not thinking straight—because if Sheila-not-Shelly drops by while we're out, she'll want to know why Martha isn't supervising us. Best to get where we're going and get back quick.

Best to take the van.

It's only a few minutes past two o'clock when I pull up in front of Darlene's, but Sissy's pacing out front.

"Bye!" she says to Darlene as she climbs in. "What took you so long?"

"I'm right on time."

"You're late," Sissy says "We have to hurry. Did you buy Lester's food?"

"Yeah, and Martha wants us to get some burgers."

"We have to feed Lester first," Sissy says. "He hasn't eaten since yesterday."

"Fine."

Lester wolfs down that stinky can of food while Sissy kneels there watching him. That beast sure can eat. It's so windy that Annie's stuff is flapping around inside the storage locker. I pull the door most of the way down. No sign of the Old Fart on his three-wheeler.

"Lester's still hungry," Sissy says. "Did you bring another can?"

"No. Do you think Annie's hiding any money in here?"

"No stealing," Sissy says.

"I'm not gonna steal anything. But if your Gramma Annie hid some money and we found it, we could pay her rent. So she won't get kicked out. You gonna help me look?"

Sissy shakes her head.

"Maybe you don't remember," I say. "But the Old Fart told us that if she didn't pay up, he was breaking her lock and selling all her stuff."

I start looking around, and Sissy finally joins in because I'm "messing up Gramma Annie's things."

Some people hide money under their beds, but this lady has no bed. There's not enough room to lie down on the carpet so she must sleep in her chair. It's got one of those handles on the side that tip it back. And with the wind rattling the door like it is today, it must get cold and noisy in here—day *and* night.

Sissy looks at a bunch of junk on the bookshelf.

"Look, Soli," she says. She pulls out a big brass key on a piece of yellow yarn. "Is this the same as the one Annie gave us?"

I hold the two keys together.

"Nope."

"Maybe it fits that box," Sissy says, pointing to a wooden box on top of the bookshelf too high for her to reach.

I check the box, but it's not locked. It's got letters inside, and they're all from Marine Sergeant William Simmons. They're addressed to Mrs. Annie Simmons at a post office box in San Francisco. The envelopes are open so I take a look. Just letters, no money. I look closer at the brass key under the light of the hanging bulb. It has the letters "USPS" stamped on it.

Sissy looks too. "What's it mean?"

"United States Postal Service?"

"Maybe Annie has more letters."

"Yeah," I say. "And maybe her mail has some cash in it."

Sissy takes a letter with Annie's post office box number on it and the brass key, and we lock Lester in. We drive to a post office on Twenty-third Street, but there's no box with that number, so we try the one on Bryant Street. Jackpot. It's stuffed with mail to Annie, some advertisements and bills. The personal letters are all from Sergeant William Simmons.

"We'll open these and see if he sent any money," I say. "So we can pay her rent."

"No," Sissy says, hugging the letters tight. "We have to give them to Annie."

So I'm stuck driving us to the hospital. I plan on telling Annie her rent is past due. I'll give back her storage locker key. She can take care of everything herself from now on.

That old lady smiles when she sees Sissy, like Sissy is her great-granddaughter.

"We checked on Lester," Sissy says, "and we brought you your mail."

Annie reaches for the letters with her shaky old hands.

"Bless you, dear. Look, they're from William. He's so thoughtful. I haven't heard from my William in a long time," she says.

Maybe if she checked her mailbox she'd hear from him more often.

Sissy pulls up a chair and sits close to Annie. "Want me to open one for you?" she asks.

"Yes, dear, would you please?" Annie says.

"Which one's first?" Sissy asks.

Annie says she can't read William's crooked writing without her glasses. Sissy's not too good at reading either.

So it's up to me to read William's letters. But first Sissy makes me put them in order. I read the oldest one first. Looks like Annie hasn't picked up her mail in a couple of months. William, he's off with his marine unit overseas, and he can't say where. "Loose lips sink ships," he writes.

The first couple of letters are all friendly and "how's it going with you and Lester?" No money or checks inside either.

"Isn't that nice?" Annie says.

Sissy opens the next letter. I read faster so we can get out of here. Now William is worried about his mom, and why doesn't she write? Why haven't the last two checks he sent to the apartment manager been cashed?

"Mom, I hope you're okay," I read aloud.

"William's always worrying," says Annie. "Me and Lester are doing just fine."

Sissy's eyes get big as I read the next letter. William wants to know what happened in that little apartment he rented for her?

"The apartment manager wrote me and said there was a fire in your unit and that you haven't been back to the apartment since," I read aloud.

"Mmm," says Annie.

We're all silent.

Waiting.

"What happened?" Sissy asks.

"Just a little fire," says Annie. "What else does my William say?"

"Mom," I read aloud. "Please write and tell me you're okay. I need to know what happened. Love, your son William."

Annie lets out a big sigh. Sissy does too.

"I used to send him brownies," Annie says. "William loves pecan brownies, but I don't bake much anymore."

Maybe because she doesn't have an oven to bake in, or an actual kitchen, and oh, yeah—a real place to live.

I fold up the letter and put it back in the envelope. I look at Sissy and make eyes toward the door, but Sissy's not paying attention.

"I was baking brownies when the fire started," Annie says. "Next thing I knew Lester was meowing and the smoke alarm woke me up. I put Lester in his basket and we hightailed it out of there. Lester hates the sound of fire engines."

"Speaking of Lester," I say. "He's waiting for you. Are you getting out of here today?"

"No," Annie says. "But this is a nice place to stay. Very warm and comfortable, you know. And free food."

"Did you know your rent's overdue?" I ask.

"My apartment rent?" Annie says. "I don't know about going back there after the fire. Where did you say my William was? He pays all the bills and takes care of everything."

"We'll take care of Lester," Sissy says. "Don't worry."

"Lester? Who's Lester?" Annie says.

"Your cat," Sissy says. "You remember Lester."

"I'm tired," Annie says. "It's hard to remember everything." She turns on her side away from us and pulls the covers up hiding her face.

If she doesn't remember her cat, I bet she doesn't remember she's living in a storage unit. So she's not going to miss it if she gets kicked out. Still, it'd be too bad if Annie and her son lost all their stuff. They've still got two good tires in there.

"Come on, Sissy," I say.

Sissy leaves the letters in a drawer next to the bed.

As we're waiting for the elevator, a doctor comes to talk to me.

"Your grandmother needs to stay at least one more night," he says. "But we need to register her. She was so dehydrated and confused when she came in. She didn't have any ID so we'll need to verify her name and—"

"Her name is Annie Simmons," Sissy says.

The doctor tries to hand me a clipboard full of forms.

"I'm not very good with forms," I say.

"Then just give us your contact info and phone number. We've stitched up her forehead, but I'm concerned about her memory. Have you noticed any confusion or memory loss?"

"Uh, maybe," I say. The elevator is taking way too long.

"We need someone to sign her admission papers and insurance forms. Is there a Mr. Simmons, your grandfather? Or someone else—your parents? We'll need her social security number and information on her eligibility for Medicare or Medi-Cal."

"Sorry, we don't know anything about that," I say.

"Where is she living?"

"Right now she lives—uh, alone," I say. "Here in the city."

"With her cat," Sissy pipes in.

"Who's taking care of you and your sister?"

I almost mention an Uncle Lester who lives nearby, but I stop myself just in time. The doctor would want me to bring Uncle Lester in. "Martha's taking care of us."

"I'll page the medical social worker assigned to your grandmother. She can help you and Martha fill out the required forms. The social worker can refer your grandmother to Meals on Wheels and other senior support services when she's ready for discharge in a couple of days."

"Uh—okay. Thanks."

The elevator arrives but the doctor waves it on. He points us to a set of chairs in the hallway and tells us, "Don't go anywhere." He says the social worker will be up in ten minutes or so.

Another social worker? No thanks.

So the minute he disappears into his office, I grab Sissy's arm and we disappear too—down three flights of stairs and back to the parking garage before I have to make up more fake relatives. That gets me thinking about Wired. Wired drove me crazy talking about his uncle in the East Bay. My uncle this, my uncle that. "My uncle is the manager at McDonalds. My uncle's gonna get me a job there."

Yeah, sure. Wired's fake uncle was about as real as our Uncle Lester-the-Cat signing Annie's hospital papers.

"I don't belong here," Wired was always saying at the Three Stooges House. "My uncle's coming to get me just as soon as he gets his new place built." Or he'd say, "My uncle would've got me for Thanksgiving, but his wife just had a baby, so they want to settle in. He's gonna come get me at Christmas instead."

No one believed it. Did Wired believe it? If Wired's uncle wanted to come get him, he would have. Either Wired made up his fake uncle, or his uncle was jerking him around and didn't want to tell him the truth. The truth was, no one was coming for Wired, just like no one was coming to get me.

Sissy's quiet in the elevator and all the way out to the parking lot, but as soon as we get in the van, she's fidgeting with her sweater pocket.

"What've you got there?" I ask.

Sissy pulls out a thin blue envelope with William's return address.

"Soli, you have to write him a letter."

CHAPTER 25

The closest burger place is back near the storage facility, which is good because Sissy only eats half of her fish sandwich and insists she's saving the other half for Lester because "poor Lester's still hungry."

"We're not going back there today. Martha's waiting."

Sissy does her silent thing. I eat my burger and ignore her pitiful looks, but the burger doesn't taste very good with her staring at me.

"You going to finish yours?" Sissy says. "If you don't want it, Lester could eat it."

"We're not staying long."

Sissy was right about Lester being hungry. Back at the storage unit, he wolfs down the beef patty and the fish but skips the buns. I look around at Annie's stuff. Maybe we could move a bunch of it to Martha's but it'd take too many trips and Martha doesn't have much space. I doubt I could talk the Old Fart into delaying her rent payment. Besides, it's not my problem.

"Let's go, Sissy."

We're ready to leave when the wind rattles the door, spooking Lester. That fat cat runs out, and Sissy chases after him down the row of storage units. She catches him right in front of the Old Fart on his three-wheeler.

"What are you doing here again?"

Sissy steps back, holding the heavy cat, as the old guy putt-putts closer.

"Do your parents know you're hanging around here all the time? That your cat?"

"Yes," says Sissy, hugging Lester tight.

"We just came from the vet," I say. "We're on our way now. We got what we needed."

"Good," he says. "Because there's no pets allowed here. Did you tell your aunt her rent's overdue?"

"Yeah," I say.

I can't do anything when Sissy climbs in the backseat of the van with Lester. I lock the storage unit and start the engine. I figure we'll do a lap or two until the coast is clear, then put Lester back where he belongs. But after two laps, the Old Fart is still sitting there on his three-wheeler in front of Annie's storage unit. He's got his arms crossed in front of his chest, so he doesn't seem in any mood to discuss an extension for Annie's rent. We have no choice but to bring Lester to Martha's house. How are we going to get that humongous cat past Martha?

No problem. When we get back, Martha is spaced out, sitting on the couch with her bum leg resting on a pillow on the coffee table. She's not even watching TV, just staring at the wall.

"Hi," Sissy says. Then Sissy speed walks right past Martha with that fat, lumpy Lester cat tucked under her sweater. And Martha? She doesn't notice a thing.

Sissy's getting sneaky good. I say hi to Martha and hand over her burger. I check on Chance, and he's taking a nap in his crib. I take the papers I'm supposed to fill out for the second day of my job workshop and tap on Sissy's door.

"Close the door, quick," she whispers. She's disconnected one room from her cardboard dollhouse, and now she's tearing up newspaper.

The cat is sprawled on Sissy's bed, licking his outstretched paw like he's always lived here.

"This can be his bed or a litter box," Sissy says. "But Soli, he needs water."

I go to the kitchen, tuck a plastic bowl under my shirt, and get a cup of water. Martha hasn't even started on her burger yet. Just as I hand the cup and bowl over to Sissy the doorbell rings.

I poke my head out to see Martha limping to the door.

Bad news.

It's not just one social worker. It's two. And one of them is that cranky, rule-book-following, allergic-to-cats Sheila-Not-Shelly.

"Sissy," I say. "You have to hide the cat."

I need to hide my file better—or figure out how to get it back in the social worker's stuff without anyone noticing. But with two social workers watching? Impossible.

don't have time to think up a new place to hide my file, so I keep it in my closet. Chance wakes up and I watch from the hallway as Martha brings him into the living room where Karen—my old social worker—sits down on the couch next to Sheila-not-Shelly.

Sheila ignores me as usual. I stand in front of Sissy's room, trying to look natural, like I'm not blocking her door. She's hiding in her closet with the cat.

Karen sees me, nods my way, and says, "Hi, Soli."

"Hi."

They look like they're here to talk to Martha, not inspect our rooms, or talk to me or Sissy. Karen's talking in a calm, quiet voice while Martha holds Chance on her lap and rubs his little arms. Martha keeps standing up, sitting down, and shifting her body around like she can't get comfortable. Chance doesn't look comfortable either.

Sheila-not-Shelly sits with her back stiff and straight, and she's clicking her pen over and over. She's not writing anything down, and she's not saying anything either—like maybe Karen's in charge. That's good.

I take a few steps forward so I can hear.

"You know placements like these are temporary," Karen says.

Who is she talking about?

Martha sways a little. "But Ch—Thaddeus is doing great now. Just look at him," Martha says. "A big change could slow his development."

Martha sits down again and rocks Chance. He's calm now. Martha's the one that looks upset.

"And it'd break Sissy's heart," Martha says, "if she got placed where they didn't treat her like she deserves."

Sissy's right behind me now, listening too.

"You've done wonders for both of them, Martha. And for Soli too," Karen says. "But it looks like we might have found an ideal family for Thaddeus—a good fost-adopt situation. The potential mother is a nurse, and they're looking for an infant for permanent placement."

Sissy tugs on my shirt and whispers, "Are they taking Chance away?"

"I don't know. Maybe."

"Did they find me a mama?"

"Shh—listen," I say, but I'm having a hard time listening myself. My ears are buzzing, and my hands are starting to sweat.

"I just wanted to tell you what might be coming up. We should know more in the next couple of weeks," Karen says.

Martha's rocking and rocking like it's just her and Chance, the last two people on earth.

The phone rings, startling everyone. I answer and it's Joanne, the job workshop lady. At first I think she wants to tell Martha I was late to class. I start to pretend it's a wrong number, but Joanne is all excited. She's glad she reached me. She asks if I have a pen, because she found the perfect job shadow for me.

"Tonight," she says.

Martha and the two social workers stare at me.

"Are you still there?" Joanne asks. "Do you have a pen?"

"Yeah."

Then she tells me how she's arranged "a great match" for me to do an informational interview, especially with my interest in "automotive career paths." She tells me how lucky I am, how the moon and stars must be aligned just right, because a friend of a friend of hers is a waitress at an Italian restaurant in North Beach. And they have valet parking.

My lucky night? Moon and stars aligned? Job-Lady Joanne is lucky she can't see me rolling my eyes.

"Write down this name," she says. "Mario. He's your contact. Dress nicely, show up at six o'clock, and ask for Mario." She spells out the restaurant name and makes me repeat the address on Columbus Avenue.

"Okay, six o'clock," I say. "I'll be there."

"You never know," she says. "This might lead to something."

I hang up.

"Everything okay?" Karen asks.

I nod. "Yeah. It was the teacher from my job training class."

"We'll let ourselves out," Karen says. Martha still looks dazed. Sheila does not say good-bye, but at least she stops clicking her stupid pen.

"Sheila or I will be in touch with you as soon as we know more," Karen tells Martha. "Take care now."

Martha doesn't say good-bye.

"Martha?" Sissy says after they leave.

But Martha doesn't look up. She doesn't say a word. She acts like she doesn't even know we're there. She starts humming that low-down song I heard her sing before.

"Come on, Sissy," I say.

I put Martha's still-wrapped burger into the fridge. We leave Martha and Chance alone and I read Sissy a book. She chooses the one where the bunny keeps running away, and the mama bunny keeps finding him. But Sissy's not paying attention. She twists her braid around and around, and pets Lester. He's spread across her lap like a big old purring blanket. Sissy pets that cat and looks like she's lost in her own worrisome world.

A little later the phone rings again. It's Karen.

"Soli, did I hear you needed to be somewhere by six o'clock? Because I'm still in the neighborhood and I'd be happy to give you a ride."

CHAPTER 27

I tell Sissy to keep the cat hidden and that I'll be back in a couple of hours. I explain to Martha where I'm going, grab my notebook and handouts, and meet Karen out front.

"Hop in," she says. "How you doing, Soli?"

"Okay."

It's a little weird that she's waiting around to give me a ride. Is she checking up on me?

"Where to?" Karen asks.

I give her the address on Columbus. I ask about her hybrid car. She asks me about my job training class.

"Yeah, tonight I'm supposed to shadow a guy named Mario. Follow him around on his job as a parking valet. Ask him how he likes it. Find out what kind of benefits he has. Stuff like that."

We're heading downtown about to cross Market Street when Karen brakes suddenly. Market Street is swarming with bicyclists. Hundreds of them—whooping and hollering, blowing horns, dinging bells, whistling, and flying by. I roll down my window. A long-haired bicyclist pulls a trailer with speakers blasting "Born to Be Wild."

"What's happening?"

"Critical Mass—a big bike ride the last Friday of every month," Karen says. "Amazing, huh?"

"Yeah."

Our light is green, but two guys block us with their bikes. Noisy cyclists whir by—people in costume, kids on the backs of their parents' bikes, wild-looking low-rider bikes, a gigantic tricycle, a naked guy, normal-looking people—even a bike cop in uniform rolls along. One cyclist hands a yellow rose to an old lady at a bus stop.

"What's it called again—Critical What?"

"Critical Mass," Karen says.

The signal changes. Cars honk but we're still stuck.

"Why do they do it?"

"Many reasons. Cars usually rule the road, but there's power in numbers when enough people come together and join the ride."

A woman bikes by with an orange sign: Cycling Against Oil Wars.

"And I guess some are making a statement," she says.

"Looks like a big party to me."

"That too."

The mass of cyclists thins, and the two guys blocking our intersection hop on their bikes. The back of one guy's shirt states: Share the Road. The other guy's: Stuck You.

Our light turns green again and Karen finally crosses Market Street. It seems like we just witnessed some kind of wild dream.

By the time we get to North Beach the fog is rolling in big-time. I close my window. I should have brought my sweatshirt. Karen looks at me and sighs deep. Her expression switches from all friendly to serious, like she's shifting gears on a steep hill.

"Soli, I'm doing all I can to get Sheila to back off, but I can't guarantee anything. Sheila's got something against Martha, I don't know why."

I tug at my seat belt because it's rubbing my neck.

"What's that got to do with me?"

"She's aiming to cite Martha for anything out of compliance, maybe even try to shut her down."

"So what can I do about that?

Karen exhales and taps the steering wheel. "Do you have any idea what happened to her missing files?"

"She brought a ton of papers with her," I say. "She probably mixed them up."

"It'd be good if those files turned up again, if you know what I mean."

We better get to that Italian restaurant soon because Karen's acting like she knows more than she's saying.

"I'll let you know if I find anything," I say.

"Good," Karen says. "Sheila's hard to deal with, I know. She's new to the job, maybe trying too hard to impress her boss, and anxious about her three-month probation."

"Probation? What'd she do wrong?" Now this is interesting. I watch Karen's face to see if she's hiding anything.

"Nothing. Most jobs have a probation period."

"Oh."

That's news to me. I thought only kids at juvie and parolees got probation.

Karen asks me for the address on Columbus again and slows down.

"Listen, Soli," she says. "You can't mess up. Martha can't mess up. If you want to keep living at Martha's you've got to be careful."

She pulls over to the curb in front of an Italian restaurant. A sign on the street says: Valet Parking. A tall guy in a white shirt and blue vest comes up to Karen's window.

"No thanks," she says to the valet. "I'm just dropping him off."

Karen reaches into her purse and pulls out her business card. "I'm writing my cell number on the back," she says to me. "Call me if you come across those files, okay?"

"Okay," I say. "Thanks for the ride."

I get out. Karen waves and drives away. I put her card in my pocket and walk up to the tall guy in the blue vest. His nametag says, *Valentino*.

"I'm looking for Mario," I say.

"Mario's not coming in tonight. Who the hell are you?"

CHAPTER 28

I'm shivering in the fog, trying to explain. Looks like Mario never told Valentino I was coming.

"So you intend to just stand around and watch? What kind of dumbass idea is that?"

"It's for a summer job workshop." I open my notebook. "It's uh, an informational interview. I ask you questions about how satisfied you are with your job."

"And Mario agreed to this? That's the stupidest thing I've ever heard. You want to know how satisfied I am? We're supposed to have two guys minimum on each shift. Three or four guys on a busy Friday night. I need a runner. You're it."

Valentino hands me a blue vest and matching ball cap.

"Put these on. Hurry up. What did you say your name was?"

"Soli."

"Soli, huh?" He taps the plastic nametag on my vest. "Tonight you're Mario."

I have no time to argue because a Mercedes pulls up and Valentino says, "Zip up your vest, Mario, before my uncle Angelo sees your shirt. You know how to drive, right?"

"Yes, but—"

Valentino cuts me off. "Keep quiet around the customers, pay attention, and do what I say." He grabs my notebook and tosses it on a little shelf inside the valet sign.

"Good evening, sir," Valentino says. The driver and his wife get out and hand Valentino their keys. Valentino gives the man what looks like a ticket stub and slides into the car. He waits for the couple to walk into the restaurant, then he parks the Mercedes in front of a fire hydrant.

"Keep your eyes open for any legal spots," Valentino says. "Or the cops."

I watch as Valentino locks the car, puts a prenumbered section of the tag under the windshield wiper, and writes the make and license number on the remaining stub, along with the street address where it's parked. He attaches the stub to the key ring, and hooks it all onto the back of the valet sign. The back of the sign has numbered hooks that match up to the numbers on the stubs. There's already a row of keys.

Another customer comes out of the restaurant and hands me a tag.

"I'll help you, sir," Valentino says and he grabs the tag from my hand. He matches the number on it with a set of keys hooked on the back of the sign. Then he tosses me the keys to the Mercedes. "Pull the Mercedes into the spot I'm vacating," he yells.

What choice do I have?

Valentino pulls a Volvo out from a legal space in front of the Mercedes he just parked at the hydrant. I hop in the Mercedes and roll forward about five feet. I wish I could drive it farther. I like the feel of the soft leather seats and the quality of sound coming from the stereo speakers. It's not my kind of music, but the lady singing a sappy song in Italian or Greek or something sounds pretty smooth. I glance in the rearview mirror and see the Volvo owner handing Valentino a five-dollar tip. Valentino stuffs it in his pocket. I can already see how this job might have its advantages.

It gets busy after that. At first Valentino makes me stand there while he drives most of the cars. But when it gets hectic with people coming and going all at once, he makes me double-park the cars until he's free to drive off and find other parking spots. Of course he pock-ets all the tips. I start estimating what he's stuffing into his pocket, but I lose track around a hundred and fifty bucks.

Then Valentino gets preoccupied with his cell phone. Sounds like he's fighting with his girlfriend or ex-girlfriend. So I get to park more and more cars. I like checking out the interiors, figuring out which switches do what. But it's getting stressful. Valentino barks orders at me, and he manages to step forward every time the owners are giv-ing tips. He keeps it all. We've got a whole row of double-parked cars now and we're clogging the street.

Then he says, "Stand here. Don't do anything stupid. If someone comes, just take their keys, give them a tag, write down the make and model of the car and keep double parking unless you see a legal spot on this block. I'll be back in a little while."

Valentino hands me a pen and a stack of blank tags. He drives off in a white Lexus. I'm left standing in the cold, while the fog turns to drizzle.

A police car cruises by.

"You're blocking traffic," the cop shouts. "Get those vehicles out of here."

"Yes sir," I say.

Where's Valentino? I move toward the sign with all the keys on the back, pretending I'm going to grab some keys and start parking the cars somewhere else. But I can't leave the cars or the keys un-attended, especially since they all have tags spelling out exactly where they're parked. What if someone like Wired came along? One of those cars would be gone in no time.

Luckily the cop rolls on.

After that I don't even have time to think because Valentino's still not back and customers are coming out of the restaurant wanting their cars. The first wave of people are no problem. They're all parked right on the block. I jockey some nice cars in and out of parking spaces, putting the double-parked cars in the freed-up spots. My parallel parking skills come in handy.

"Nice maneuvering there, Mario," one guy says as he hands me a tip. His date is looking me up and down. I like how the wind is blowing her clothes, and the way she doesn't even bother trying to hold her skirt down. She just laughs and jangles the gold bracelets on her wrist. I hold her door open.

"Thanks, cutie," she teases, as she slides in—all long legs, low-cut blouse, and perfume filling the air. I can't help looking. I don't think I'll write that job benefit down on the informational interview form, but it's a nice one all the same.

Valentino's still not back, but I've got a smile on my face and money bulging in my pockets. So he can take his time as far as I'm concerned. The owner of the restaurant brings me an umbrella because the fog-turned-drizzle is starting to feel like rain.

The owner mumbles to himself and watches me as I carry the sign off the street and under the awning. I pull another car into the space where the sign used to be.

"Where's Valentino?" he asks.

"He'll be right back," I say, even though Valentino's been gone at least twenty minutes.

The owner says something about his idiot nephew and leaves me in the rain.

I'm making good tips now, especially each time I walk customers to their cars with the big umbrella. I don't have time to count how much, but I'm thinking I've got to hide my money before Valentino gets back. I might have enough to pay down the two hundred and seventy-five dollars I owe Martha for my bus zone burrito ticket. Or maybe I can give some cash to the Old Fart at the storage place so Annie and Lester won't get kicked out. If I write to her son, he'd pay me back, right?

Two couples come out. They're all laughing and tipsy. One guy hands me a stub with numbers on it. I match the numbers to a set of keys on the board. Valentino has scribbled an address on Filbert Street. I have no idea where Filbert is. We're on Columbus, that's all I know. All the other cars were parked or double-parked on Columbus.

"Hey kid, what are you waiting for? You gonna get my car or not?"

"Yes sir, in a moment. I just have to wait for Valentino to get back."

Problem is, Valentino never comes back.

CHAPTER 29

Those people complain to Angelo, the owner. Angelo storms out of the restaurant with his cell phone and starts leaving messages in English and Italian for Valentino, calling him his "idiot nephew." If I were Valentino getting those messages, I wouldn't be in any hurry to return.

I try to leave but Angelo grabs me by the vest.

"Where do you think you're going?" he asks.

"My mom and my sister are expecting me. I was only supposed to interview Mario, then go home for dinner."

"Mario? I should have known. My other idiot nephew," he says. "But you're not going anywhere. We got customers. The customers, see—they want their cars. What do you want?"

Angelo is a big guy and he pulls me halfway down the block, trying to talk in a low voice so the people waiting for their cars can't hear.

"What's your price, kid? You got me by the meatballs. So what do you want? You want a nice dinner on the house for you and your girl-friend? You got it. I don't trust my idiot nephews. They're both fired. I don't know you, but whoever you are, I gotta trust you. Now go get these people their cars, okay?"

"Okay, but—"

"But what?" Angelo shouts. He's pulling me back toward the restaurant.

"But I don't know where Filbert Street is, or any of the other streets Valentino wrote down. And I can't leave the keys or the double-parked cars unattended, even if I did know all the street names."

"See? You're already smarter than my lousy nephews. Filbert? You want Filbert? No problem. I got a map. And I got a busboy, Mike. I bet Mike knows all the streets. You can work together."

Angelo whaps me on the back. "Come on, we're getting wet," he says. Then Angelo tells the people waiting, "See? We got it all straightened out. No problem. He didn't know where Filbert Street is. That we can fix."

Next thing I know, me and a busboy named Mike are working together and pocketing cash like I never imagined.

I'm running and sweating like crazy, checking my map, driving through wacko intersections with six streets all coming together, some of them one-way—usually not going in the direction I need to go. The drizzle lets up a little, turning to drifts of fog, but I'm still searching for the windshield wiper switches in all the cars. I get a crash course in North Beach street names while I try not to hit pedestrians crossing to the restaurants, outdoor cafes, bars, and strip clubs. People are walking every which way, looking like they're having fun, judging by how they're not paying much attention to traffic.

All the cars with stick shifts seem to be parked on the steepest hills. I drive a Maserati—an unbelievably smooth Maserati—up one hill so steep, all I see is sky. When I reach the crest, it's a dead end. A view of San Francisco Bay spreads out before me between patches of slow-moving fog, with boats on the water and the bridge all lit up. I want to sit and stare—pretend for a while this car is mine—that I live in one of the apartments nearby with a big-screen TV glowing in the window. But I have to roll backward downhill, turn without hitting any parked cars, and hurry to the restaurant to give the car back to its owner. Then go fetch more cars.

And it's not just the bridge that's lit up. Bars are lit up, and cafes—and a bookstore called City Lights. Nearby, a neon sign in the shape of a woman's figure glows in front of a club called La-La-Lola. Two well-placed, blinking red lights distract me so much, I start going the wrong way up a one-way street—right in front of a cop. Luckily the cop's staring at flashing La-La-Lola too, so he doesn't see me make a quick U-turn.

Hours zip by as I run around and navigate my way back to the restaurant. I'm making good tips and getting hungrier every time the restaurant door opens, sending garlicky smells of good Italian food wafting into the street. I have no idea what time it is, and when I realize it's nearly midnight, it's too late to call Martha. She and Sissy and Chance would be asleep already.

It finally stops drizzling, and I can see a huge moon through the mist. Maybe Job-Lady Joanne was right about the moon and stars being aligned.

A waitress comes out and asks, "You boys hungry?" She's carrying two plates piled high with spaghetti and meatballs, and garlic bread on the side. I wolf it down, still standing outside. I've never tasted such good food—another job benefit.

We're down to one set of keys on the board. Mike returns to the kitchen with our plates and I have to do something with the valet sign. I bring the signboard with the last set of keys into the restaurant. The waitress tells me the keys belong to Angelo's Ferrari. So I'm looking for Angelo. The place is almost empty but I don't see him—just one burly guy, slurring his speech and telling the bartender a boring story. I grab my blank notebook, sit at an empty table near the bar, and study Angelo's map. I try to figure out which bus can get me back to the Mission District. I hope they run this late. Maybe the bartender will change some of my ones and fives for twenties so it doesn't look like I'm carrying so much cash. I don't want to get jumped.

But I can't count my money in the open either. What if Valentino shows up and tries to take it all? I guess I made enough to pay Martha for part of the bus zone burrito ticket and make some kind of payment to the Old Fart so Annie won't lose her storage locker.

My belly's full of good food. My pockets are full of I don't know how much money. I'm feeling some serious "job satisfaction" as Joanne the Job Lady would say. So I'm not expecting the big guy at the bar to turn into an angry drunk and start yelling at me.

"Where's my Lexus?" he shouts. This is bad, especially when the last set of keys on the signboard aren't his. I panic. How could I have lost a whole car? Then I remember the car Valentino drove off in—a Lexus.

"If you don't get my Lexus here pronto," he yells. "I'm calling the police. What's your name?"

"Mario," I say.

CHAPTER 30

Angelo must've heard the screaming. He comes out of the kitchen.

"Hey Mike, call Mr. Sobbrazzi a cab, will you?" Angelo says. "You're in no state to drive, Mr. Sobbrazzi. We don't want you running over any tourists. That'd be bad for business."

The cab comes quick and Sobbrazzi stumbles out the door. Mike tells me that Sobbrazzi's a regular and Angelo calls him a cab at least once a week when Sobbrazzi's had too much to drink. Maybe that's why Valentino took the Lexus, thinking no one would notice it was gone until morning.

Angelo sees me studying the map. "Hey kid, you need a ride home?"

"I can take the bus," I say. "Thanks anyway." I take off the cap and vest and hang them over the signboard.

"Where do you live?"

"In the Mission."

"I can drop you off at BART on Market Street. How's that?"

"Thanks."

In his Ferrari on the way to the subway station, Angelo starts griping about his nephews again. "Valentino took off in Sobbrazzi's car, didn't he?"

"I don't know," I say. "Maybe something happened to him?"

"Sure, kid. More like a new girl *happened* to him. That boy can't think straight when he's got a new girlfriend."

I don't say anything. I just look out the window as we pass through

Chinatown. The streets are starting to make sense to me. We'll be downtown at Market Street in just a few minutes.

"What's your name? I know it's not Mario."

"Soli."

"Okay, Soli, you got a clean driving record? Because maybe we could use you."

I'm thinking my driving record must be clean because I don't have my license yet—so no driving record is a clean driving record, right? But Angelo's no dummy. He can tell something's up because I hesitate.

"Bad record?" he asks. "You're undocumented? Illegal alien, what? Tell me. You using someone else's social security number?"

We're stopped at a light and he's looking at me. "I've seen it all, kid. What's up with you? You want a job with Angelo? Then you got to be straight with me."

Do I tell him I've been driving expensive cars at his restaurant all night without a license? He'd check my DMV record before he'd ever hire me for real. He'd find out—one way or another. The light turns green and Angelo makes a right onto Market Street.

"You don't want a job, eh?"

There's that moon again, smaller in the sky than it was before, but full and round.

"Yeah," I say. "I want a job. But, uh, I wasn't expecting to be parking cars tonight. Just interviewing Mario or Valentino for my summer job class."

"What are you saying?"

Angelo passes one BART station and continues down Market.

"I'm saying you asked me to get the people their cars."

"Yeah, so?"

"So I wanted to help out."

"Yeah, you helped out. And you made good tips, right? Now I owe you and your girlfriend a nice dinner on the house."

"I don't have a girlfriend. Maybe I could bring my little sister instead?"

"Fine. Bring your sister, bring your mama, bring the whole family. Bring granny and pops. So what's the problem?"

"The problem is I want a job, and I like parking cars. But I have to be careful. I can't mess up. And right now—uh—I don't exactly have my driver's license. So if I get caught without a license, that'd mess up my—uh—living situation."

"Now you tell me. So, Soli, between you and me, we'll just keep quiet about you parking cars in front of my restaurant tonight, okay?"

"Okay," I say.

Angelo's careful of the handful of cyclists in the bike lane as he pulls over to the BART station at Powell and Market. The cyclists move on, their red taillights blinking in unison. I'm surprised how many people are still out this late. The Powell Street cable car operator pushes the cable car around on its turntable so it faces the other direction. Tourists climb aboard.

"So when're you going to get that license?" Angelo asks.

I'm ready to open the door and run in case Angelo flips out, or wants my tip money back.

"When I turn sixteen," I say.

"When's that?"

"About ten months from now."

I'm expecting Angelo to get mad, but he doesn't.

"You remind me of me, when I was your age," he says. "Gutsy, and flying by the seat of your pants. I started working when I was twelve.

But now, you gotta be sixteen—work permits and all that. So call me when you turn sixteen and you've got your driver's license, okay?"

"Okay."

Angelo unlocks my door with the power switch.

"In the meantime," he says, "we'll discuss the busboy business. So bring your family for dinner. On the house."

"Okay," I say. "Thanks for the ride."

"You're all right, kid." Angelo gives me a fake shove out the door. "Goodnight. Go home. Get out of here."

"Goodnight."

I get back to Martha's and I'm beat. I put the key in the front door. I plan on counting my money. Then sleeping late. Not too late though—because now I've got questions for Joanne about getting a work permit.

But the light's on in the living room, and Martha's stirring herself awake on the couch. She's been waiting up for me, and she's mad.

CHAPTER 31

Do you know how late it is?" she says. "Why didn't you call?"

"Sorry, Martha, I kind of got a job for the night and it got busy."

"You couldn't stop and look for a phone? I was worried. And so was Sissy."

"By the time I saw a phone, it was midnight and I didn't want to wake you up."

"Soli, I wasn't sleeping. Next time, call."

"Okay," I say.

Martha's too tired to lecture me very long, which is good because I'm too tired to listen.

Martha drags herself up and limps off to bed without even saying good night.

I count my money. Two hundred and seventy-one dollars!

Next morning, Martha barely gets out of bed. She feeds Chance and Sissy, but she stays in her pajamas and robe all morning. She doesn't look so good. I'm worried so I skip my class.

I make me and Sissy some peanut butter sandwiches for lunch, using up the last of the bread. Martha feeds Chance, but I haven't seen her eat anything since yesterday morning. Her uneaten burger is still in the fridge. One minute her face looks pale, the next it's flushed.

"You okay, Martha?" I ask. "You want your hamburger?"

"No thanks, I'm not hungry," she says. "I'm just gonna put Chance down for his nap. Then take a little rest myself," she says.

I feel bad she stayed up late waiting for me. Plus I never picked up Martha's medicine that day Sissy and I ran over the nails.

"Martha, I can go to Walgreen's on Mission and get your medicine. You need it?"

"No thanks, Soli. I just need to catch up on my sleep."

"I'll take Sissy to the park," I say. "That way it'll be quiet for you and Chance."

Martha says, "Okay," like she's hardly listening. She usually tells me to walk Sissy to Dolores Park, but she's not saying anything, just humming a little while she rocks Chance in her big old chair.

I'm supposed to lay off the driving, but I have to give the Old Fart some money for Annie's storage unit or she'll be living on the street. And it's time to take Lester back to Annie's storage place, where he belongs. Sissy refuses to hide him in her sweater though. And when I try to pick him up, he hisses at me.

"You're scaring him," Sissy says. "Leave him alone."

So Lester stays in Sissy's room while we go pay a visit to the Old Fart. We park in front of his office.

"What are we going to tell him?" Sissy asks.

"Don't worry," I say. "I got some money to pay Annie's rent."

"Did you steal it?"

"Of course not. I earned it on my job last night."

Sissy looks impressed. We go in and I give the guy one hundred dollars in fives and ones. He counts it twice.

"A hundred dollars," I say.

"She owes ninety-six more."

"Yeah, but that's what she's paying now. You want it or not?"

He puts the money in his pocket.

"We need a receipt. And a copy of Annie's records showing what she paid so far."

"Who wants to know?"

"Her son, William. He's coming to town and he told me to check."

"Humph," says the Old Fart, but he writes us a receipt.

"One hundred cash," he says. "You have to come back for a statement of her balance. My bookkeeper only comes in once a week."

"Thanks," says Sissy.

We're driving back to Martha's. Sissy's going on about how happy Annie and William are going to be. I think I'll send him a letter to tell him where his mom is and that he owes me a hundred bucks. Maybe he'll give me an extra reward for making sure they didn't get evicted. Sissy and I are both feeling good, but when we get back, we find Martha sitting exactly where she was before. At least she finally changed out of her pajamas. Chance is fussing in his room. His voice is getting louder.

I check on him, and except for one of his little shudders, he looks okay.

"Hey buddy. How's it going?" I ask him. "Did you have a nice snooze? Martha's not feeling so good. I hope she's not getting sick."

Chance reaches up for me and I carry him past Sissy's closed door. Sissy's in there talking to Lester and Lester is meowing back. When I get to the living room with Chance, Martha says, "Soli, my leg's burning up and I'm feeling a little dizzy. Can you drive me to the clinic? We'll take everybody in the van. Then you drive back and watch over Sissy and Chance, okay?"

I know her knee must be real bad, because she never leaves me with the baby. It's against the foster rules. Of course she's not supposed to leave me with Sissy either.

So we all drive to S.F. General—me, Martha, Sissy, and Chance. I pull up to the white zone and ask Martha if she wants me to park so we can go in with her.

"No, no," she says. "I'll just walk on in. You take the kids home and keep them safe, okay? I'll talk to my specialist. They probably just need to give me some stronger ointment for my knee. I'll call you to pick me up when I'm done. Shouldn't take more than a couple of hours. There's a bottle in the fridge if Chance gets hungry."

Martha gets out slowly. She winces when her feet meet the ground. It takes her a minute to get steady. Then she adjusts her purse, takes a breath, and turns around to look at us.

"You all be good now," she says. "You can ask Mrs. Morrow next door if you need anything. And if anyone calls, just tell them I'm in the shower and I'll call them back. Okay?"

"Okay," Sissy and I say, and we watch her go.

I don't like the way she's walking on a slight tilt, deflated. Reminds me of driving around on our spare tire. Like the air that's supposed to be holding us up is gone.

CHAPTER 32

We're not even back in the door yet when Chance starts crying and the phone starts ringing. That was quick.

I look in the fridge while Sissy runs to the phone.

"Ask her how she heats the bottles," I say.

"Hello?" says Sissy.

She runs her finger through the curly phone wire coming from the handset.

"Yes, uh-huh. Sorry, she's in the shower right now."

Uh-oh, it's not Martha. I move noisy Chance farther from the phone and start humming to calm him down.

"Oh, okay. Uh-huh. Sure. Okay, bye." Sissy hangs up.

"Who was that?"

"Darlene's mama."

"And you told her Martha's in the shower, right?"

"Yeah," says Sissy. But she's twisting her braid now just like the phone cord, so I know something's up.

"What?"

"Darlene's coming over," Sissy says.

"What? Are you crazy? Why's she coming here?"

"Martha told her mama that Darlene could come over anytime. And Darlene's mama has to go to the airport to pick up her daddy. So Darlene's coming here."

"Why didn't you tell her this wasn't a good time? Why didn't you tell her Martha was feeling sick?"

"I told her Martha was in the shower, and she said Martha could give her a call if there's a problem. Otherwise if Martha doesn't call, she's bringing Darlene in fifteen minutes."

"Martha can't call, so now what are we going to do?"

Chance cries louder, and Sissy looks like she might cry too.

"Okay, okay," I say. "We'll just call her back and tell her it's not a good time. Where does Martha keep her phone numbers?"

"In her purse," she says, "the one she took with her." Sissy bites her lip.

I pull out the telephone directory.

"What's Darlene's last name? We'll look it up."

"It starts with a *M*," Sissy says. "I don't know all the other letters." Sissy takes a couple of steps back.

"Okay, what's that phone code—star something? Where it automatically calls people back?"

Sissy shrugs. Big help she is.

I flip through the customer guide in the front of the directory. There it is—call return—star-six-nine. Martha won't like the extra charge but there's nothing I can do about that.

"Okay, Sissy, come here. I'll press star-six-nine and that'll call Darlene's mama back. When she answers, you say today is not a good day."

Sissy nods, all serious, and stands next to me—ready to talk to Darlene's mama.

I press star-six-nine, and it starts ringing. But that's all that happens.

Their phone just rings and rings.

CHAPTER 33

I send Sissy next door to ask Mrs. Morrow to come over, but Sissy comes back alone.

"Nobody answered," Sissy says.

If Darlene's mama sees Sissy and Chance and me unsupervised she might get Martha in trouble. A violation like that, and Sheila-not-Shelly could shut Martha down.

"Sissy," I say. "Darlene and her mama are on their way over here right now. So I'll feed Chance, take him in his room, and close the door. You tell them the baby is going down for his nap and Martha's rocking him to sleep, okay?"

"That's a lie," she says.

"You told them Martha's in the shower. Were you telling the truth then?"

"No, but Martha told us to say that," Sissy says.

"Well, now *I'm* telling you what to say. Do you want Martha to get in trouble for leaving us here alone?"

Sissy shakes her head.

"Okay, then you tell them Chance is going down for a nap. And Martha can't come to the door."

Sissy stares at me.

"Chance is going to take a nap eventually, so that's not a lie, right?"

Sissy nods.

"And Martha can't come to the door right now, can she? So that's not a lie either. If you don't want Martha to get in trouble, then you got to tell them."

"Okay," Sissy says.

It's not easy feeding Chance his bottle with Sissy telling me what I'm doing wrong every step of the way. I'm not sure I got his bottle warm enough, but he's sucking it down quick so it must be okay.

"You gotta tilt him up after he drinks," she says.

"He's fine," I say, but Chance is getting fussy.

"You better change him," Sissy says. "So he'll be dry. And put Martha's special lotion on his bottom. He likes that."

I'm just about ready to change his diaper when he cries, spits up a bunch of sour milk, then gurgles and smiles at me.

"I told you you're supposed to keep him tilted," she says. "You made him burp up."

I have to change his clothes and my shirt. He's finally clean, fed, and happy again. Just in time too, because the doorbell's ringing.

I hide out in the baby's room and think about how I could buy Martha an answering machine if I got a job at Angelo's restaurant. If we had an answering machine, we could have avoided all this.

Darlene's mama only stays a minute. I hear Sissy and Darlene say good-bye, then the door closes and she's gone. Sissy and Darlene go into Sissy's room and start fussing over Lester.

I carry Chance into the living room, turn on Martha's oldies station, and sit down in Martha's chair. Next thing I know Sissy and Darlene want to fix Lester some dinner and dress him in Chance's clothes. They sort through a pile of his baby clothes in the living room. Lester likes the can of tuna fish just fine. He's licking his chops and cleaning his face after he eats, kind of prissy for such a big cat. But he's not too pleased with their dress-up game.

"Let's put Lester in the stripy pajamas," Darlene says.

"No," says Sissy. "He likes the bunny shirt best."

Sissy holds that fat cat while Darlene pulls a yellow baby shirt over his head.

"Are you sure he likes to play dress-up?" asks Darlene.

"Yes. It's his favorite."

"How do you get his arms through the holes?"

Lester finally squirms free and darts away with the girls chasing after him. He runs into Sissy's room.

"Soli," Sissy shouts. "He won't come out from under the bed!"

I don't blame him.

"Leave poor Lester alone," I say. "Find something else to do."

Chance is smiling and grabbing my pointy finger. He's pretty strong for such a little guy.

"Yeah, you agree with me, right, Chance?"

Chance bounces his body a little. He's happy. I put him in his bouncy seat and he watches what's going on.

Sissy and Darlene drag her cardboard dollhouse and all her paper people into the living room.

"You made these?" Darlene asks. She doesn't look too impressed with Sissy's cardboard dollhouse or cutout dolls. Curly would have called Sissy's weird paper people a blended family for sure, and Curly would've wanted to discuss how everyone felt about that. And like the guys back at the Three Stooges House, those cardboard people aren't talking much either. Sissy's just moving them around, setting them up in different rooms while Darlene watches.

Darlene takes a long time to choose a cardboard doll, but after a while they're both cutting out more people and gluing them onto cardboard, moving them around the dollhouse, talking, playing, and singing along with the radio. "The ants are my friends, they're bowling in the wind. The ants are a'bowling in the wind."

I know they're singing the words all wrong, but I'm not going to tell them. Besides, this is the first time I've ever heard Sissy sing.

Everything's going smooth when Darlene asks, "Where's Martha?"

"She's in the shower," Sissy and I say in unison.

"She sure takes long showers," Darlene says.

A few minutes later Darlene and Sissy are fighting.

"You're cutting all jaggedy," Darlene says.

"No, I'm not! You're the one cutting the sisters crooked," says Sissy.

"Who cares?" I say. "Play nice like you were before."

Too late. The girls are shrieking at each other and it's upsetting Chance. He's making that pucker face and shaking his fists like he's ready to cry.

That dumb cat comes slinking out from Sissy's room carrying a dusty old sock in his mouth. He sounds weird. He's trying to meow with his teeth clenched around that sock. Sissy and Darlene chase him again and he leaps up, sock and all, onto Martha's bookcase above her TV, knocking over dusty photos of her old foster kids, and rattling all her little junky things up there. A ceramic goose starts wobbling, and I jump to catch it before it falls. Too late. The goose falls to the floor and breaks into a million pieces.

"Uh-oh," Sissy says.

"What are you going to tell Martha?" asks Darlene.

Chance is crying a real holler now. The cat tiptoes around some other dusty knickknacks, drops the sock, then starts coughing something terrible.

"Lester's choking!" Sissy shouts. "Do something!"

I doubt you can do the Heimlich maneuver on a choking cat—even if I could I can't reach him. I try to shoo him down, but it's not working. Chance is turning red and screeching now too. The cat stretches its neck making choking sounds. Louder and louder.

"Lester's having a hair ball," Darlene shouts.

The phone rings and I'm glad, because I'm ready to pick up Martha. I just have to get Chance to stop crying, keep Lester from choking to death, hide that cat somewhere, and sweep up the mess. Then we can go get Martha—right after I figure out how to explain to Darlene how Martha got out of the shower and down to the hospital.

CHAPTER 34

That crazy cat finally stops coughing and stretches out on Martha's shelf between a ceramic mouse and an old teapot. Sissy's talking on the phone, and I carry Chance into his room to change his diaper before we go get Martha.

That calms him down. He stops shaking his fists and looks right at my eyes when I talk to him.

"You miss Martha, huh buddy? Yeah, Ma-Ma-Martha. You like that, huh? She'll be here real soon. I bet that's her on the phone right now. We're gonna go get her."

I carry Chance back into the living room to do some damage control on that broken goose.

"I told Darlene's mom it was okay," Sissy says.

"What's okay?" I ask. "Wasn't that Martha?"

Sissy shakes her head.

"It was my mom," Darlene says. "Daddy's plane was late, then they switched him to another airport—my mom's driving there now—so I get to stay over, until eight o'clock tomorrow morning, Mom said."

Sissy stands there stiff as can be, lips closed, not saying a word—just slowly blinking her eyes at me.

Darlene grabs Sissy's hand, swinging their arms back and forth together. "We're having a slumber party!" she says.

I have a bad feeling in my stomach, and it gets worse when Lester makes the weirdest yowl I ever heard and starts coughing again. He hacks up a glob of stinky, slimy tuna mixed with fur and other disgusting stuff right down the front of Martha's color TV.

"Eww!" scream Sissy and Darlene as they go running down the hall.

The phone's ringing again.

Sissy and Darlene come chattering back.

I grab the phone.

"Hello?" I say.

"This is Sheila Lupano from the Department of Social Services. Let me talk to Martha."

Sissy sits on the floor near me, crosses her legs and pats her lap for me to put Chance there. I slide Chance into her lap and motion for her to shush.

"Martha is in the shower right now," I say into the phone.

"Still?" Darlene whispers to Sissy.

"I can give Martha a message," I say. "And she can call you back."

"Look, I'm heading out soon," the social worker says. "Tell Martha to call me on my cell. I'm coming tomorrow at ten and I need to talk to her before then."

I write down Sheila's number on the notepad Martha keeps on the phone table.

"Does Martha know what the visit's about?" I ask.

Sissy's sitting on the floor with Chance in her lap. She's singing and cooing, smiling at him, and rubbing his head nice and soft. Darlene's holding both of his little feet in her cupped hands like they're the most precious things she's ever seen. Chance likes all the attention and he's got a goofy smile spreading across his face.

"Karen informed Martha on our last visit. It's happening quicker than we expected, but . . ." Sheila exhales and her voice is impatient. "Look, just tell Martha to call me, and to have Thaddeus packed and ready to go at ten tomorrow morning. I'm taking him to his new family."

CHAPTER 35

F or a minute I feel like punching a hole in the wall, but I can't.
So I take some deep breaths like Curly back at the Three Stooges
House told us. And I pace back and forth while I wait for Martha to
call. It's been three hours since we dropped her off. I've got to keep
busy, so I sweep up the broken goose, clean the cat barf off the TV,
and check the fridge.

Sissy says, "Lester's hungry."

"He's fine," I say. "We don't need any more cat vomit."

"He needs dry food like Oprah, the hamster. It'll make him feel
better."

Lester's not the only one who needs food. Martha's refrigerator
is looking pretty pitiful. Just a few bottles of Chance's formula and a
big hunk of cheese. Martha didn't touch her burger. I pry apart the
soggy bun. The tomato and cheese are congealed together, the lettuce
is droopy and it doesn't smell right. I toss it and check Martha's money
jar. It's near empty. I need some fresh air so I take her last few dollars
and some of my tip money and we all roll Chance in his stroller down
to the corner store. Sissy wants to bring Lester along, but I won't let
her. We got ourselves a little parade as it is. We buy a small bag of cat
food, a carton of milk, and a loaf of bread. And we pick up an empty
cardboard box for another litter box, because the one Sissy made is
soggy and stinking up her closet.

"Don't you need kitty litter?" Darlene asks.

Sissy sees me counting the dollars and says, "Lester likes torn
newspaper. It's fresher for him."

When we get back to Martha's, I make Sissy and Darlene clean up their dollhouse mess while I heat up another bottle for Chance. He sucks it down fast. Sissy tells me how Martha usually mixes up Chance's baby porridge with a little bit of formula and a mashed banana. We're out of bananas, but Chance eats the baby cereal pretty quick.

Sissy and Darlene giggle at the mess he makes. When the phone rings again I'm hoping it's Martha, but my heart is telling me it's more bad news. I don't even want to answer.

It's Martha.

"How's Sissy? And did you find Chance's bottles? Ask Mrs. Morrow to come by and help you," Martha tells me.

"Mrs. Morrow's not answering her door," I say.

"Soli, I know I shouldn't have left you with Sissy and Chance. But I didn't have the heart to call social services—they'd cart you all off to different places in the middle of the night."

"Yeah," I say. "So the doctors are taking care of you?"

"They gave me painkillers, but my leg's infected." She sounds tired and far away. "I'm on an antibiotics IV and I'm . . ."

There's a silence and I'm waiting for her to say more. But she doesn't.

"Martha, you there?" I ask.

Silence.

"You're coming back, right? Martha? And Chance—he—we need you."

I don't know what I'm saying but I know I have to tell her about Sheila coming to take Chance.

"Soli, I'm depending on you," she says.

"Martha, that social worker called."

"Who—Karen?" she asks. Martha sounds drifty and her voice is fading.

"No, not Karen," I say. "Sheila, that mean one, and she says she's coming to take Chance away."

"Hold on . . . ," Martha says.

"Martha, listen," I say. I have to ask her what to do about Chance, and Darlene.

"The nurse is, wait—yes, I'm feeling okay now, thanks." Martha's talking to someone else. "Wait a sec—Soli?" Martha says. "She wants to—uh-huh . . ."

"Martha, you there?"

"Hello?" It's a strange lady's voice.

"Where's Martha?" I say. "Who's this?"

"This is the nurse. Martha's pain killers are kicking in so she needs to rest now."

"I've got to tell her one more thing."

"I'm sorry. She's sleeping."

"Sleeping? When can she leave?"

"The doctor will decide that. Visiting hours start at nine," she says. "You can talk to her then."

"Nine tonight?"

"Nine tomorrow morning."

"Tomorrow?"

CHAPTER 36

I burn my thumb making grilled cheese sandwiches. Sissy and Darlene gobble them down. Lester eats his dry food and laps up his water, then climbs back up on the bookcase while Sissy and Darlene draw pictures. The girls start fighting because they both want the orange crayon to draw Lester. So I break the orange one in half.

Chance drinks another bottle. What if we run out before tomorrow?

"What time does Martha put Chance to bed?" I ask. He doesn't look sleepy. I'm holding him and he's trying to grab my nose.

"After his bath."

"His bath?"

"Yeah, you've seen Martha. She gives him a bath in the kitchen sink."

I look at the sink full of dishes and the greasy grilled cheese pan.

"Where *is* Martha?" Darlene asks.

Sissy and I don't say anything.

"She's not in the shower, is she?"

Sissy and I still aren't talking.

"Is Martha dead?" Darlene looks like she's gonna cry.

"No, no, Martha's not dead," I say. "She's just resting up."

"At the hospital," Sissy says. "Just for a little while." Sissy pats Darlene's back. "We'll take care of you. Right, Soli? And your mama and daddy will come get you in the morning."

I know how Darlene feels. I've been left a lot of places myself. And I don't remember anyone coming to pick me up, or patting my back all tender like Sissy's doing. Sissy lets her hand rest awhile each time she touches Darlene. I've seen Martha pat Sissy the exact same way. Chance and I go sit next to them and I help pick up her cardboard people.

"Thanks," Sissy says. She reaches over and pats my back—her little hand staying there a heartbeat or two, before she lifts it up and pats again. Like there's something invisible but real holding us together.

I spread a blanket on the living room floor. Sissy and Darlene keep an eye on Chance while I clean up the kitchen. They're showing him Sissy's favorite paper dolls and singing to him so he doesn't feel lonely.

Even after I get the plates and bottles humming in the dishwasher and the kitchen is all cleaned up, I'm not sure about giving him a bath. The sink looks cold and hard, and I'm afraid he'll bump his head. So I bring some warm wet washcloths and a fluffy dry towel over to where Chance is safe on the blanket, and we wash him up that way. Then we put him in a fresh diaper and clean pajamas.

"This is better than dressing up Lester," Darlene says.

"Chance is all shiny and clean," Sissy says. "And we helped."

"Yeah," says Darlene.

Darlene and Sissy don't want to take a bath, which is fine with me. Next thing I know they drag more blankets and pillows out of Sissy's room and set up a little slumber party on the living room floor. Sissy's wearing her sweater over her pajamas, waving her favorite nightgown at Darlene to try on.

"No thanks," Darlene says. "My T-shirt's comfy." She gets under a blanket, wiggles out of her jeans, and scrunches them under her pillow. Sissy gets under the blankets too. "Aren't you going to take off your sweater?" Darlene asks.

"Oh yeah," Sissy says, and struggles to get it off while Darlene watches.

"What happened to your arms?" Darlene says.

Sissy pulls her elbows back quick and her arms disappear under the blanket. "They got hurt," she says.

"Does it still hurt?"

"Not anymore," Sissy says. "Because Martha rubs her special lotion from the Scarlet Sage store on them. Every day, Martha says—a little bit every day—her lotion's gonna make my scars fade away."

"How about today?" Darlene's face is close to Sissy, and she's looking right into her eyes. "Did Martha rub some on you today?"

Sissy shakes her head. "She had to go to the doctor."

"I could do it."

"Okay," Sissy says, then she's up getting the lotion.

I hold Chance and watch as Darlene pours the lotion into her palm, then rubs her small hands over Sissy's outstretched arms. First one arm, then the other.

"Smells like flowers and honey," Darlene says.

"Yeah." Sissy nods. "Martha says it has healing herbs and flower petal oil in it."

Maybe Chance can smell it too. He relaxes his body, leaning back against my chest, as Darlene takes her time swirling that lotion back and forth on Sissy's arms.

After that, I read them book after book with Chance down on the blanket listening too. Even Lester jumps down from his perch and cozies in.

Darlene falls asleep first, her hand still petting Lester. Lester doesn't seem to mind. He's lying on his side, a low rumble of a purr coming out of him. He sounds like the motor humming on one of those expensive cars at Angelo's restaurant.

Sissy whispers all tender to Chance, face to face. She gently rubs his head until Chance's eyes blink more and more slowly while he looks at her. I'm thinking I have to tell her that Chance is leaving tomorrow. I have to tell her that Chance has a new family, and she's got to tell him good-bye. Only I don't know how to say it.

So I just watch them until they're both asleep, then I look up at Martha's ceiling light until its blue and green colors blur.

I adjust the blankets on Darlene and Sissy, and I pick up Chance real careful so he doesn't wake up. I carry that little guy close to my chest, and I can feel his warm cheek against my neck. He's a little drooly but he fits just right in my arms and the weight of him feels real and heavy, and I hate to put him down. So when I get to his room I sit in Martha's rocking chair and lean back with Chance sleeping on my chest. I pat his back and cover him with one of those little blankets Martha has, and I rock him and talk to him even though I know he's already asleep. He doesn't need any rocking right then, but I do.

I tell him about the church songs I remember someone singing to me, but I can't remember who. And some lady folding yellow and blue towels. How I loved sitting in her laundry basket and feeling those warm towels, fresh from the dryer, and how they smelled so clean. I tell him about sitting in a foster mom's shopping cart at the grocery store and how I'd laugh when she waved the wet lettuce over my head saying, "It's raining! Oh, it's raining!" Then I'd get a kiss on my forehead.

"I don't remember who she was, Chance, I can't even remember her face, but I remember laughing with her. You're going to have your own mama now, and you'll get to remember."

Chance keeps sleeping while I talk. I tell him the good things I remember, but I don't tell him any of the bad. I rock and rock. I haven't cried in a long time and now I use the corner of Chance's baby blanket to wipe my eyes.

"Don't worry, Chance. None of that bad stuff's going to happen to you."

When I put him in his crib, he lets out a little sigh in his sleep like he's relieved we've had this talk.

I'm exhausted when I fall into bed. I don't know how I'm going to tell Martha and Sissy about the social worker coming the next day. It seems like I've just closed my eyes when someone's tugging on my arm.

"Wake up," Sissy says. "Something's wrong with Chance."

CHAPTER 37

"C ome on," Sissy says. "He won't stop crying."

I'm half asleep but I'm out of bed and I can hear Chance wailing. Sissy's dragging me down the hall.

"I sang to him," she says. "But then he started crying again. I can't reach inside his crib."

"Okay, okay. Don't worry."

Chance is worked up, shrieking and shaking his little fists. I lift him out of there, hold him against my chest and pat him on the back, but he's still whimpering and making big gasping baby cries that shake his whole body.

"Maybe he's wet," Sissy says and gets a dry diaper ready on the changing table. I change him but he starts hollering even louder.

"Hey, buddy, don't worry. You're okay. Let's get you a bottle."

The clock in the kitchen glows 2:10 a.m. Darlene is still sleeping with Lester next to her so we leave most of the lights off and I just click on the light above the stove. I heat up the last bottle and Chance finally stops crying while he sucks that down.

"He was hungry," Sissy says.

"Yeah, I guess so."

I sit in Martha's big chair and hold him while Sissy sits on the floor and rubs his leg. He's not as scrawny as he used to be, and his stretchy pajamas are starting to fill out and fit him snug and tight. Chance kicks his little feet while he drinks the rest of his milk. His eyes follow my voice, then Sissy's.

"Is that lady going to take him away?" she asks.

"Yeah, I think so. Tomorrow morning."

"Is he going to get his own mama?"

"Yeah."

"Are they taking you away?" Sissy whispers.

"No, I'm sticking around."

"Good," she says. "Can I hold him?"

"Sure," I say, and I let Sissy take my place in the big chair. I put Chance in her lap, and he's smiling and falling asleep at the same time. There's a little milk dribble on his cheek.

Sissy's holding him and rocking back and forth.

"Is he gonna have a nice family?" she asks, looking up at me.

"Yeah, you heard Karen. His new mama wants him forever. She'll take good care of him."

"And give him lots of love?"

"Yeah."

"So that's a good thing," she says, her voice trailing off to a shaky whisper. She tilts her face down until her cheek nuzzles the top of his head. She breathes in deep. "So that's not sad. He's going to have his own mama. A mama who loves him."

"Yeah," I say again.

"Soli, can I hold him a little longer?" she asks.

"Sure."

I read the instructions under the stove light. I wash my hands, mix up a batch of his formula, and fill the clean bottles from the dishwasher. I get a whole shiny row full of bottles ready for him in the fridge. Then I lift Chance from Sissy's lap and she follows me back to his room.

I'm ready to put him in his crib, but Sissy whispers, "Wait, I need to give him a good-night kiss." I lean down, close enough for her to reach him, and she kisses him on the cheek.

"You too, Soli," she says. "You need to give him a kiss."

I kiss him on top of his head and I put him back in his crib.

"Soli," Sissy whispers, "you think I'll ever get my own mama?"

She looks so serious, like her whole life depends on my answer. But I can't lie to her.

"I don't know."

We're both quiet. We can hear Chance's little baby sighs, breathing in, breathing out.

"Little Sister, you've been waiting a long time for a good mama, haven't you?"

"Yeah," she says.

"While you're waiting, you got Martha and me."

"Yeah," she says again.

CHAPTER 38

I want to sleep in, but Chance is howling for food before six in the morning. The girls wake up, and now everyone's hungry. Sissy and Darlene eat Cheerios and milk. Chance drinks a bottle, and I feed him more baby cereal. That little guy has a big appetite.

Lester eats more dry food, then he drags one of Martha's yellow rubber gloves on top of the bookcase and bites holes in it.

I'm tired and hungry. I sit at the table holding Chance, and just as I'm pouring milk on my cold cereal, the doorbell rings. It's not even six-thirty yet. Who's up this early?

"Who is it?" Sissy calls through the door, just like Martha taught her.

It's Darlene's mama and she's an hour and a half early.

"Get your jeans on, Darlene," I whisper. "Sissy, don't open the door yet. Wait till I take Chance to his room."

But Darlene can't find her jeans in the mess on the floor. She's hopping around all excited to see her mama—and she opens the door before I can get away. I want Sissy to say good-bye to her friend quick, but Darlene's mama pokes her head in.

"Sorry to come so early—oh, hi—I just wanted to say hello to Martha and thank her," she says. She comes all the way in, leaving the door ajar. "Darlene, get dressed, baby doll. Daddy's waiting and he's tired."

Darlene gives her mama a quick hug, then rummages through the stuff on the floor. She dredges up Sissy's sweater and hands it to her.

Darlene's mama looks around. "Where's Martha?"

Sissy hugs her sweater to her chest.

"She's resting up," I say.

I'm tired of saying she's in the shower. Chance burps up a mouthful of baby cereal on my shirt. Then he smiles.

"So you're watching the girls and the baby?" she says, all fake friendly. Then to Darlene she says, "Darlene, hurry up now. Where are your clothes? Don't keep your daddy waiting."

"Is Daddy mad?"

"No, but he's tired and hungry, so let's get going. Come on now."

Two forceful knocks push the door open and Darlene's daddy comes in.

"What's taking so long?" he says.

"Darlene's just getting dressed," her mama says. Darlene moves closer to her mama. Now they're both looking for her jeans. "Where'd you take them off, baby doll?"

"Right here," Darlene says.

Sissy looks back and forth between Darlene and her daddy, then she sets her sweater down and helps them look. I go to the sink with Chance and try to wipe my shirt. Darlene's daddy is staring at me and he's weirding me out.

"Where's your mother?" he says, coming closer.

"They're foster kids," Darlene's mama whispers to him. "Remember?"

Sissy glares at them. I don't like how Darlene's mama is whispering either—like we can't hear every word she's saying.

"Martha's tired," I say. I go back to the table with my bowl of cereal.

He narrows his eyes and inspects Martha's glass jars of herbs on the shelf above the stove. If I keep my mouth full of food, maybe he won't ask me any more questions. But he catches me between bites.

"So you're watching the kids while she sleeps?" He stares at me until I have to answer.

I nod and say, "Your Darlene and Sissy get along good together." I dip my spoon in, ready for his next interrogation question.

Darlene finds her jeans and pulls them on. Good, now they can leave.

"Okay, Sissy," I say. "Tell your friend good-bye."

"Bye," says Sissy.

But Sissy and Darlene just stand there.

"Where are your socks?" Darlene's mama asks her. "Check Sissy's room. Hurry up now."

Darlene's daddy keeps looking around.

"Where'd you say your uh—foster mom, this Martha was?" Darlene's daddy says. Maybe he thinks if he talks loud enough, he'll wake up Martha and she'll have to come out.

I'm too tired to think up a story. I just want to eat my soggy Cheerios.

"Darlene, where's Martha?" he asks.

Chance makes his pucker face and his lips and eyebrows start to quiver. Darlene starts sniffling, maybe because his voice is scary, or maybe because her mama is jamming her shoes onto her feet without any socks.

"No need to cry," her mama says, even though she looks like she might join her any minute. "Come on now, everyone's tired. Let's just go home."

"We're not going anywhere until I know where Martha is."

"Stop yelling at them," Darlene's mama says.

I don't like the way he's shouting or how she's talking all pitiful about us.

"Martha had a doctors appointment this morning, " I say. "I'm picking her up right after breakfast."

"You just said she was sleeping," he says.

"I said she was tired." I stir my soggy cereal.

"Darlene," her mama says. "Martha watched over you last night, right?"

"No," Darlene says. "Because first Martha took a long shower. Then she had to stay overnight at the hospital. Soli made us grilled sandwiches. He read us stories, then we slept in the living room. We had a slumber party."

"She means Sissy and Lester and her," I say. "Not me. I slept in my own room."

"Lester?" Darlene's daddy says.

Darlene points at the bookcase.

"Lester's a cat," I say.

Darlene nods.

"But Martha wasn't here?" Darlene's daddy acts like he's a cop on some bad TV show. "You were alone with Darlene—with both girls—overnight? Without any adult supervision?"

Sissy tries to pull her friend away, but Darlene crawls under Martha's little telephone table instead. Sissy backs down the hall, clutching her sweater. She looks like she's heading off to her bad-dream land. This guy better stop.

"Yeah," I say. "But nobody planned it that way. That's just how it turned out."

He starts yelling at Darlene's mom. "I can't believe you left Darlene here overnight."

This is bad. What if Sheila finds out? Chance is wailing now. He doesn't like loud voices.

"Where's my cell?" Darlene's daddy pats his pockets but can't find it. "I'm calling the cops."

"Calm down," Darlene's mama says, but he's pacing back and forth.

"Everybody's okay," I say. "Nothing bad happened."

I don't blame Darlene for hiding. Her mama is bending down, trying to cajole her out while her daddy's acting crazy.

"Darlene, get out of there," he shouts. When she doesn't move, Darlene's daddy pounds his fist hard on the kitchen table. My plastic bowl goes flying and lands upside down—milk, spoon, and cereal all over the floor.

Now Darlene's crying along with Chance. I'm glad Sissy's hiding somewhere.

Moe at the Three Stooges House could take this guy down, but not me.

"Darlene, what happened here last night?" her mama says. Then she points at me. "Did he—did something happen?"

"Whoa, you got it all wrong," I say.

Sissy's next to me again, clenching her sweater.

"Yeah," Sissy shouts. "You're wrong, wrong, wrong!" She's screeching louder than when she was yelling jujitsu stuff at that tow truck driver. Then her arms pick up momentum, until she's swinging her sweater back and forth, whacking Darlene's daddy's knees—hitting him with her sweater again and again. Not that she's hurting him any. But he's shocked. Me too.

"Get out of here and leave us alone!" she shouts, still whomping on his knees. "And we're not *foster* kids. We're kids living in a foster home!"

Everyone stares. She's impressive. Darlene's daddy looks like he doesn't know what to think, but he backs up toward the door.

"Sissy," I say.

Sissy drops her sweater on the floor. She's suddenly silent, like maybe she just realized how big Darlene's daddy is. She stands right next to me again, breathing hard.

When Darlene peeks out to look at Sissy, her mama reaches for her, yanks Darlene out from under the table, then notices the pad near the phone. "Social worker—ten o'clock? What's this?" she says.

I move toward the table and reach for the pad. Too late. She's got the pen and she writes Sheila's number on her hand.

Darlene's mama and daddy make serious faces at each other.

"We don't need you calling any social workers or any cops either," I say. "Martha had a medical emergency. She thought the doctor would take care of her quick and she'd be back in an hour. She didn't know she'd be hospitalized—or that you'd drop Darlene off here. Besides—you're the ones who left your kid overnight without even talking to Martha."

"Maybe so," Darlene's mama says. "But something's not right here. Sissy, you're coming with us. I'm going to find out exactly what happened here last night."

"Tell them, Soli," Sissy says.

"What?" I say. Sissy's tugging on the back of my shirt like we're both drowning. I take a breath. "Nothing bad happened."

"Yeah," says Sissy.

I feel like shouting at them, but Chance is clinging to me, taking shaky little breaths, looking up at me like he's trusting me with his whole little self. So I take another breath and keep my voice steady—not too loud, but firm.

"I watched over your Darlene," I say, "just like I watch over Sissy and the baby here. Like Martha does—I made sure your Darlene had dinner, that she was safe, and that she didn't feel abandoned while you were gone."

Darlene nods her head. Sissy too.

"So you don't need to report Martha—or us—to anybody."

I'm talking faster. I don't know what I'm going to say next, but they're listening.

"Just like you got a family and you care so much about your Darlene—we got a family here too. Martha's making our lives better. She takes care of us—like we're her real kids—so we don't need you and your wrong ideas messing that up."

"Yeah," Sissy says. She stands by me, tugging on my shirt—and with Chance clinging to me too—it's like we got our own little Critical Mass happening.

It's quiet for a minute. No one says a word. Darlene's mama and daddy look at each other like they got some secret silent language. Feels like we're all stuck at a four-way stop, waiting to see who'll roll into the intersection first.

It's Lester. He rolls off the top of the bookcase—goofy cat—and lands on his feet with a thud. "*Meowp*." Lester runs down the hall dragging Martha's yellow glove.

Darlene's daddy tromps out and I work it out with Darlene's mama. She's going to take Sissy for a couple of hours. I'm keeping Chance with me while I get Martha.

"If I don't hear from Martha . . . ," she says—and she flashes me the number on her hand.

"Martha'll call you," I say.

Sissy doesn't want to go with them. She looks up at me and Chance.

"It's okay, Sissy," I say. "You can go with Darlene for a little while."

"You're going to come get me. Right, Soli?"

"Yeah, you'll see me soon," I say.

"Then I gotta say good-bye to Chance," she says.

I sit down holding Chance so they're the same height. She puts her face close to his, and he grabs her hair. Sissy gives him a kiss on his cheek.

"Bye, Chance," she says.

Sissy follows Darlene and her mama out the door, but then she runs back. Sissy cups the baby's face in her hands, and looks right into his eyes.

"Don't forget me, Chance. I won't ever forget you," she says. "I'm your first big sister."

CHAPTER 39

O kay, Chance, now it's just you and me," I say.

Lester rubs against my legs and *meowps*.

"Okay, you and me and Lester."

Lester sniffs the floor, then starts licking up milk and Cheerios. That's less for me to clean up, so I leave him to it.

I give Chance another washcloth bath, change his diaper, and get him dressed in his little outfit with the cars on the shirt. I pack extra clothes and his favorite fuzzy yellow duckie in his baby bag. I think about packing up some more supplies and driving off with Chance in Martha's van so Sheila can't take him. I'm not ready to let him go, even if he's got a new family waiting for him.

It's just after seven o'clock, so I have time before visiting hours at nine. I put Chance in his bouncy seat, shoo Lester into Sissy's room, take Annie's son's envelope from Sissy's desk, and stick it in my back pocket. I stack up all the blankets and books in the living room, then I move on to the kitchen.

Lester did a pretty good job on the floor. Chance watches me as I wipe a dishrag over the remaining milk and soggy cereal. It's not as good as Martha would do it, but it's good enough. I put the milk away and the doorbell rings. Maybe Darlene's family forgot something. It's too early for Sheila-not-Shelly, but I'm not risking it. I pretend no one's home but whoever it is won't go away. The doorbell keeps on dinging.

The doorbell scares Chance and he's scrunching up his face to cry. I can't remember if I locked the door when Sissy left, so I tiptoe over and double-check. I attach the chain too—as quietly as I can.

"I can hear you in there. Open up!"

I step back and try to make my voice sound like I just woke up. "Who is it?" I say, even though I already know.

"Sheila Lupano from social services."

Darlene's mama must have called.

I rumple my hair to look like I just got out of bed. I open the door a crack, but I keep the chain on.

"I thought you weren't coming until ten," I say with a fake yawn.

"Let me in," she says. "I need to talk to Martha."

"Martha's still sleeping. She wasn't expecting you till later."

"Unlock the chain," she says.

"Martha told me never let anyone in unless she's awake. Martha works hard—she's up late with the baby, and she needs her rest."

"Look, go tell her I'm here."

Look yourself, lady.

I close the door and lock it. I'm stuck and I need time to think. I grab a couple of Chance's bottles from the fridge and tuck those into his bag. I could climb out the window with him but then Martha would get in big trouble. Besides, where would we go?

Sheila's pressing nonstop on the bell again.

I have to figure a way to keep both me and Martha out of trouble and keep that awful Sheila away from Chance. I have an idea.

I open the door again and leave the chain on like before.

"Well?" she says. "Where's Martha? And don't tell me she's in the shower."

"No. No, she's not in the shower. She's in the bathroom, though. And she's not coming out anytime soon, if you know what I mean."

"What's wrong with her?"

"She's sick. Upset stomach. So if you want to come back at ten like you said last night on the phone, that'd work out better."

"I'll wait."

"Suit yourself. I'm going back to bed." I try to close the door but she puts her pointy shoe in the crack.

"I know you're up to something," she says. "I read your file."

"My file? I heard you lost my file. Not very responsible of you. You're lucky Martha doesn't report you to your supervisor, make an official complaint or something."

"Are you threatening me? I'm not stupid you know."

"Me?" I say. "No, I'm not threatening you. I'm just saying if you come back at ten, or eleven, or even better—at noon—I bet Martha will feel so much better that she'll probably forget all about reporting how irresponsible you are for losing any files. Come to think of it, Martha might have found something important when she was vacuuming under the couch yesterday. Since you got plenty of time to wait, let me go check."

Sheila-not-Shelly tries to peer in the gap between the door and the frame. I pick up Chance in his bouncy seat and move him down the hall out of sight.

"Hope this works, buddy," I whisper to him. "You think I got a chance?"

He waves his arms at me and smiles. I hand him his rattle toy to keep him busy. I get the brown file from my bedroom closet, pull a few things out for safekeeping, and go back to the front door.

"Yep, here it is," I say through the gap. "You're lucky Martha keeps everything so clean and safe here. Someplace else, a file like this might've stayed lost and collecting dust balls for years."

"Give me that," she says.

Whoa, this lady still doesn't know how to say please.

"Then you'll come back at noon, right? When Martha's feeling up for a visit?"

"Yes," she says. "Hand it over."

I give her the file. She doesn't even say thank you.

"Look, I've got the file now, and I'm not going away,

"You just gave away your only bargaining chip. Clearly, you don't know who you're dealing with."

"You look, uh, Shelly. I have a question."

"It's Sheila, not Shelly."

"Right," I say. "What makes you think I'm so stupid? Clearly *you* don't know who you're dealing with."

She's silent.

"You know, I have a question about something weird in that file of mine. I noticed there were three different—let's see, what were they called?—'site visit reports,' signed by you and Martha. They were dated in April and May."

She doesn't say a thing, but I can hear her shuffling papers.

"The strange thing is, Martha told me you didn't start visiting us until June. So I checked Martha's signatures."

"What?" Sheila says.

I peek through the gap. She's still rummaging though my file. She won't find what she's looking for, because I removed those reports, along with the ones that jerk at juvie wrote up.

"What are you saying?"

"I'm glad you asked. You see, I'm familiar with Martha's signature, what with Martha signing my school notes and all. So I'm guessing you were supposed to check on us—what, once a month? Maybe you didn't—maybe you got busy or forgot or something—so you decided to write those fake reports and forge Martha's signature to cover your tracks. Make it look like you were doing a good job when you weren't?"

Sheila's not saying a thing.

"You still there?" I ask her.

No response. But I can see her slowly moving papers in that file.

"Back at juvie," I say, "three strikes on probation and you'd get in big trouble. How does probation work at *your* job? Because Joanne at my summer job workshop says it's very important that your boss doesn't see you messing up, especially when you first start working. She says you never get a second chance at a first impression. Your boss might be mad if he hears that you lost my file, wrote fake reports, and forged Martha's signature. By my count that's three strikes against you."

I look down the hall to check on Chance. He's got a happy little beat going in his bouncy chair.

"What do you want?" three-strikes Sheila-not-Shelly says.

"Like I said before, all I'm asking is that you give Martha a little more time to rest up this morning. Come back at noon. And, you know, give us a little more space and respect from now on."

"So if I come back at noon," she says. "Martha won't mention anything to my supervisor?"

"Yeah, I bet she'll act like she doesn't know a thing. But you got to lay off—leave Martha alone now because she's doing a good job."

"And you'll give me the missing reports?"

"Yeah, sure."

She glares at me through the gap.

"So you won't come back till noon?" I say.

"Yes." Sheila turns around and walks away.

I close and lock the door, then peer out the window. Sheila-not-Shelly gets in her car and drives off.

"Hey buddy," I say to Chance. "We just bought ourselves a little time."

I got rid of Sheila for now, so Martha won't get in trouble for leaving us unsupervised. Martha still doesn't know that awful social worker is coming back at noon to take Chance away. And maybe I'll give Sheila one of those missing reports, but I'm not giving her all of them.

I tear up the list Sheila made of Martha's violations. If I get caught or they send me off to some other place, at least Martha won't get in trouble. I tear up the reports from that jerk at juvie. Nobody needs to see those either. I put the shredded papers inside one of Chance's used diapers and toss it in the diaper bucket. Just in case things don't turn out right, I hide Sheila-not-Shelly's forged fake site visit reports in Martha's big bad wolf book. If I get sent away, Sissy or Martha will find them eventually. I write across the top of one of them, *Martha, look—Sheila's faking these reports and forging your name. You should turn her in.*

Then I add, *Thanks, Martha. This is the best place I ever lived.*

I put Chance in his little jacket and grab his baby bag. I tear off Sheila-not-Shelly's phone number from the pad by Martha's phone. When I tear off that top sheet, I'm half-expecting to see a big thick X on the next page.

Nothing.

I've been worrying about Larry's warning—about coming across the big X for a long time now. But I've already been dealt the big X—ever since the day I was born and someone left me on that Greyhound bus.

"Isn't that right, Chance?"

Chance smiles and a trace of a shaky tremor pulses through his little body. Yeah, he's dealing with his own X too. Chance is better than he used to be, but he still needs all the help he can get.

I look out the window to make sure Sheila's not lurking around.

"Come on, Chance. Time to empty your diaper bucket. Then we're going for a ride."

Chance waves his arms like he thinks that's a good idea.

CHAPTER 40

I lock up the house, empty the trash, and get Chance buckled into his car seat in the back of the van. I toss in his baby bag and the stroller. I think again about stealing him away. But Martha and Sissy need me.

So I drive, find a spot in the parking garage at San Francisco General, and put Chance in his stroller. He likes rolling along.

The reception desk gives me Martha's room number on the third floor.

I'm inside the elevator, pushing the number three, when I realize Martha and Annie are on the same floor. The elevator door opens and I see Annie's doctor in the hallway. So I push four and pull back to the corner of the elevator so he doesn't see me.

"Fourth floor," says a nurse riding with us.

I don't have any choice but to roll us out. I stroll Chance twice around the fourth floor, trying to figure out how to see Martha without running into Annie's doctor. But Chance is too cute. The nurses and orderlies are all staring at us and making *coochie coo* sounds and smiling at him, so I head back to the elevator.

I punch the lobby button this time and head on down to the ground floor. I roll Chance around and around, thinking if Martha and Annie have the same doctor or nurse, I'll probably have to tell them about how Annie's living in a storage unit. I never had time to write her son a letter. Maybe I'll just hand over William's return address and tell them everything.

"Shifty! Hey, Shifty!"

I turn around and there's Wired.

Unbelievable. I feel a smile stretching across my face. Wired is standing behind a wheeled cart. People are waiting in line to buy coffee and tea from him.

"Hey, man. That you, Wired?" I roll Chance up to the cart.

Wired is smiling too. I wait till he's done with his customers. He's real friendly to them—a true businessman. His tip jar is half full of coins and dollar bills too.

"How you doing?" I say. Wired and I just stand there grinning at each other. I want to reach out and punch him in the arm or something, but there's the cart between us.

I don't tell Wired I'm glad he's alive and not shot dead by a bunch of cops after he's been driving stolen cars all hyped up on caffeine—but that's what I'm thinking.

"I called the Three Stooges House," I say. "Larry said you weren't there anymore."

"Yeah," says Wired. "My uncle finally came and got me."

I guess he didn't make up his fake uncle after all.

"That's great. So that's working out?"

"Nah," he says. "My uncle's a jerk. I had to call my court-appointed advocate and my social worker to ask for another placement. It took awhile, but now I'm set—I'm with a new family and they helped me get into a high school entrepreneur program. Got my own business here summers, and three afternoons a week during the school year."

"*Entre* what? You're talking big words now, huh, big shot? Whoa—you're getting rich, man." I nod at his tip jar.

"Yeah." He raises his eyebrows. "Gonna buy me a car. And who's this?" he asks. "Can I give the kid a cookie?"

"Uh, no thanks. I don't think he eats cookies yet."

"You don't know? What kind of daddy are you? You messed up big-time, Shifty."

"Whoa," I say. I hold up my hands to stop him, but Wired's doing his over-the-speed-limit talking—just like he used to.

"Weren't you listening to Larry with his 'don't do anything stupid' X-on-the-notepad-story? Your kid's cute, man, but you messed up. How you gonna do anything now that you got a kid? How we gonna take that road trip?"

"I'm not his daddy. He's like my little brother. Right, Chance?" Chance smiles at me.

"Whew," says Wired, fake-wiping his forehead. "What're you doing here anyway? He's not sick, is he?"

"No, we're visiting Martha, my foster mom, so I got to get going. Let me get your number."

Wired writes his number on a napkin and hands it to me. I do the same.

"There's a custom van and car show coming up at the convention center," Wired says. "You want to go?"

"Yeah, call me."

Wired nods.

I dread going to the third floor to tell Martha about Chance. So I stand there a little longer. It's gets kind of awkward—staring at each other—neither one of us saying a word. So I ask him, "What else is new with you?"

"I switched to decaf."

CHAPTER 41

C hance and I come off the elevator on the third floor. Old Annie's room is across the hall and there's no doctor or nurse in sight. I roll Chance to Martha's room. I knock, then peek in. I was hoping she'd be all dressed and ready to go, but Martha's still in bed.

"Hey, Martha, how are you feeling?"

"Much better now that I see my two boys," Martha says. "Where's Sissy?"

"She's at Darlene's."

"Good idea," she says.

Chance is reaching his arms out so I lift him and hand him to Martha.

"Hey there, Chance," Martha says as she smothers him with kisses. Chance is eating it up, grabbing her cheeks, and making happy gurgle sounds.

"Martha," I say.

She looks up and sees my face. She knows. She knows before I say anything.

"They're taking Chance." I have to say it anyway.

"When?" Her eyes are watery. Just watching her makes my throat clench.

"Today at noon."

It's hard to get the words out. I look at Chance's baby bag all packed and hanging on the back of the stroller. "That awful Sheila is coming to your place. She said to have him all packed and ready. I told her you were in the bathroom. I didn't tell her you were in the hospital."

"We have to let him go. You know that, right?"

"Yeah," I say. "And Sissy knows. She already told him good-bye."

I look out the window so she doesn't see my face.

"It's not easy," she says, "letting them go."

"Yeah," I say.

"I'm looking into putting some papers in with the agency," Martha says. "To try to adopt you and Sissy."

"You're going to do that?"

"Yes. But first I have to get my act together. Take care of my health, and get prescription glasses so I can renew my driver's license. I don't want to mess up and risk losing you or Sissy. How do you feel about me trying to adopt the two of you?"

"Okay," I say. I walk back to Martha and Chance, and sit in the chair next to her bed. Chance waves his arms at me.

"Just okay?" she asks.

"More than okay. But can't we keep Chance?"

"No. I tried. They found him a permanent home. We have to let this guy go with his new family."

Martha's hugging and kissing him again, and Chance is grabbing onto her hair and smiling.

"Why do you want to adopt me?" I ask. "I'm still messing up."

"Me too, Soli. Me too. But you're a good kid and you're like my own son now. You're in my heart, Soli—you and Sissy both."

"I got a few things I didn't tell you."

"Oh yeah?" Martha says. "Like what?"

I'm thinking I have to tell Martha everything, so I start with taking the van a few times without her permission, parking in the handicapped zone at Toy Mart, and how I picked up that old lady and pretended she was my grandma so I wouldn't get a ticket. Then how we ran over the nails and got two flat tires, how the police found us and made us visit old Annie, and how she's right across the hall.

"Sissy and I visited her a couple of times, then she asked us to check on her cat—and it turned out she was living in a storage unit."

"A storage unit?"

"Yeah," I say.

I tell Martha about Annie's tires, her overdue rent, how we got her mail, and how I didn't have time to write her son a letter on account of Darlene stayed overnight.

"Darlene stayed overnight?"

"Yeah," I say. "Sissy told her mama you were in the shower but she dropped Darlene off anyway, so I watched over them. In fact, Darlene's mama and daddy are kind of mad about that. So you better call them pretty soon."

"You've been busy," Martha says.

"Yeah."

"Anything else?"

"Well, Lester broke your goose and barfed on your TV, but I cleaned that up."

"Lester?"

"Annie's cat. He's staying at our house. Sissy snuck him in under her sweater when you weren't looking."

"Sounds like Sissy's been busy too."

"Yeah. And, oh yeah—I took some of your grocery cash—all of it actually. But I earned some tips the night before so I can pay you back, and I paid off part of Annie's overdue rent."

"I see."

I decide to tell her about the tow truck and Scary Mary Poppins some other time. Martha bounces Chance a little and takes a deep breath.

She's going to change her mind and get rid of me now—she'll tell social services to send me somewhere else. Maybe she won't want me anymore, but at least I've told her the truth. I feel better—like I coughed up my own big hair ball.

"Anything else I should know?"

I could tell her the gas tank is empty, the kitchen floor's all sticky, we're out of milk, and she needs to buy a new pair of rubber gloves. I could tell her about our free dinner at Angelo's restaurant, or how I never got my permit. But instead I say, "Sissy's singing now."

"Singing?"

"Yeah, she's singing. So if you want to adopt her and not me—I know she's younger and she behaves better—so you know—I'd understand."

"Soli, come here close. Listen to what I have to say," Martha says.

I listen.

"We're a family. I intend to find a way to keep both of you."

"You sure?"

"I'm sure," she says, "Besides, you still owe me two hundred and seventy-five bucks for that bus zone burrito ticket. I got a lot invested in you."

"Yeah," I say. "You're invested."

"Yes. But let's not tell Sissy until all the paperwork is filed and we're certain it's going to happen. Sissy needs a sure thing."

"Yeah."

And I'm thinking, me too. I need a sure thing. And the way Martha's looking eyeball to eyeball with me right now? That's about as sure as I ever hope to get.

"Here," she says, handing Chance to me. "Take this little guy. I have to call Karen and that awful Sheila."

"Okay," I say. "While you're at it, you'd better call Darlene's mama too."

walk Chance over to the window. We look out at the parking garage, at all the people coming and going while Martha's on the phone. I'm listening to every word. Chance is calm and quiet, like he's listening too.

"Yes, Karen, I know. It's an unusual situation. Yes, I'm okay. Thanks, knowing that you're the one taking the baby to his new family makes us all feel a little better. Yes, room three seventeen. Yes, he's all ready. So you'll call Sheila? Thanks. Okay, good-bye."

I walk back over to her.

"Karen's coming to get Chance," Martha says.

I try to say okay, but I can't. I nod instead.

"And we won't tell anybody about all the driving you've been doing, all right?"

"Martha," I say. "I probably should have told you this before, but I don't have my own permit yet."

"I kind of suspected that. My license is expired too," Martha says. "I need to pass that darn eye exam. If I don't get my license renewed soon, I'll be in big trouble. So we both better start following the rules."

"Yeah."

Martha wants to get dressed, so I take Chance for a little stroll and drop in on Annie across the hall.

"Hi," says Annie. "Where's the little girl?"

I look at my fake grandma. It's weird talking to her without Sissy here.

"I was gonna write a letter to your son. To tell him where you and Lester are staying now."

"Lester? My cat?" Annie asks. "How's he doing?"

She must be getting her memory back.

"Fine. He's doing fine," I say.

"Can you keep him . . . until my William gets back?"

"Yeah, I think so."

"Thank you, son," Annie says.

Chance is getting fidgety so I push the stroller back and forth.

When the nurse comes back in, I reach into my back pocket.

"Here's Annie's key and the address to the, uh, place where she's living. And the other key is to her post office box. And here's a letter from her son. I didn't have time to write to him about Annie being in the hospital—maybe you can contact him? You know, tell him more about her condition?"

"Annie's son is not your dad?" the nurse asks.

"No, he's kind of like, uh—a distant uncle. We're not really related, just kind of connected, you know?"

The nurse nods.

"I'll have someone look into it," she says.

I'm relieved to hand all that stuff over to the nurse, but I'm also thinking about Mrs. Luz de la Paz, my real grandmother.

"So Annie'll be okay here, right?"

"She's in good hands," the nurse says.

I turn back to Annie. "Sissy and I will be back to visit you, okay?"

Annie nods.

Then I tell them both, "I have to go check on my mom across the hall."

CHAPTER 43

I feel guilty pretending to be Annie's grandson one minute, then walking away from her the next. But I can't solve everything. I can't save everyone. I have to save me and Martha and Sissy. Not Annie. Not even Chance.

As it is, Martha and I only have a few minutes to say good-bye to him. Martha hugs him tight, sings to him, and whispers in his ear. Then it's my turn to hold him.

When Karen comes in, Martha stays in her chair and gives Chance one more kiss.

But I can't let him go.

So I carry him as Karen and I walk down the hall. Karen pushes his empty stroller and I carry Chance into the elevator, my heart sinking all the way down to the lobby. And I carry him to the front door of the hospital. Then she wants to take him.

She wants to take him away to that fost-adopt family I'll never meet, and Chance doesn't even know what's going on. He doesn't know he'll never see me or Martha or Sissy again. But he wraps his little hand tight around my big finger—like we've got this special soul brother handshake—and he's not letting go. I can't tell him good-bye because I don't want him to know.

What good would it do for him to know in his little head that he's leaving and not coming back? Is he going to remember me? Probably not, just like I don't remember my real grandmother—if that Luz lady even was my grandmother. Just like I don't remember who was rocking me and singing me those church songs when I was little, or who was raining wet lettuce over me and making me laugh. But someone was. Someone was watching over me. Someone cared about me. Just like I care about this baby-first crack baby that's gripping my finger and not letting go.

"Okay," Karen says, "we have to go now. Long good-byes are harder on everyone."

Chance still doesn't let go. So she gently reaches over and unwraps Chance's tiny hand from my finger. But she might as well have used a big sharp knife to pry us apart, it hurts so much. My throat can't squeeze any tighter, and my heart is about to bust open. I don't know how Martha can care for all these kids, then let them go. Karen puts Chance in his stroller and starts to walk off with him.

When I offer to help, she says, "No thanks, I got him."

She takes Chance and his bag full of clothes and diapers, his favorite duckie toy, and a note I tucked in there, hidden for his new family to find. It says, *We call him Chance. Please take good care of him.*

After she takes Chance away, I walk through the hospital's garden, humming traces of that old church song. I sit on a bench and stare at nothing while the sun warms my back.

When I feel a little calmer, I go back to Martha. She's waiting for me.

"You okay?" she asks.

"Yeah."

Martha's still walking on a slight tilt, but she says she's doing fine. I stand in line for her new medicine at the pharmacy. I even pay with money I earned parking cars at Angelo's.

"Thanks, Soli," Martha says. "I owe you."

I bring the van around to the passenger loading zone so Martha doesn't have to walk too far.

"This is the last time you're driving until you get your permit," she says as she pulls herself into the front seat. "We both have to stay out of trouble now, you hear?"

"Yeah."

I make sure Martha buckles up. I look both ways as we pull out, and I pay attention to all the signals. Me and Martha, we don't need any more tickets, or the attention of any authorities.

I turn up Martha's oldies station on the radio, but neither one of us is in the mood to sing along. Martha and me, we go together to pick up Sissy.

I hear the click of Sissy's seat belt and I adjust my rearview mirror. Sissy stares at the empty car seat where Chance is supposed to be. She keeps lifting her hand up and setting it down again, like she can't find a comfortable place for it to rest. It's hard to look back there.

So I look forward.

And then me and Martha and Sissy, we all head home.

Acknowledgments

Many thanks to Alison McGhee, Norma Fox Mazer, Sharon Darrow, Phyllis Root, and all my friends and faculty at Vermont College's MFA Program in Writing for Children and Young Adults. You've provided the most inspiring literary nest from which to stretch my wings.

Special love and appreciation to my mom and dad; and to fellow writers, Ellen (E.T.) Yeomans and Lisa Rabe Bose (my guide to misheard lyrics).

More thanks to my Plot Dogs, Chapters, and Re:Writers critique buddies; to Jodi Reamer at Writers House; to Abigail Samoun, Nicole Geiger, and all the great people at Tricycle Press; and finally to T.K., and my two sweet, funny, and smart young men—Kurt and Mike—you make me proud.

Dear Reader,

If you'd like to learn about worthwhile organizations dedicated to helping children and youth in foster care, make a donation, or get involved, the following websites are a good place to start.

www.nationalcasa.org
www.ahomewithin.org/donors.html
www.sfcasa.org/giving.htm
www.youthlaw.org

Thanks,

Lynn